HER DEPUTY WOLF

WILD FRONTIER SHIFTERS

MEG RIPLEY

SHIFTER NATION

Disclaimer

CONTENTS

HER DEPUTY WOLF

HER DEPUTY WOLF

WILD FRONTIER SHIFTERS

1

"Damn it. Late again." Cash smacked his palm against the steering wheel of the squad car. The transition from a star roper on the rodeo circuits to sheriff's deputy hadn't been an easy one. He'd thrown himself into the job, taking the chance at any training he could get, working to improve himself, and constantly wanting to prove to his coworkers that he was just as capable of tracking down criminals as he was of roping calves.

It only made things more difficult that his boss was Levi Morgan. The sheriff of Sheridan also happened to be twin brothers with Wade, Cash's former roping partner. Cash had thought of this as a good thing at first. It was an easy inroad into a new job after he'd broken his arm and decided he couldn't spend the rest of his life on the back of a horse. Now that he'd been at it for a few months, he could feel Levi's tough gaze on the back of his neck.

"Cash, are you still coming?" Levi's voice crackled over the radio as though Cash had summoned him with his thoughts.

"Shit." He picked up the handset. "Yeah. I'm on my way."

"Everything okay?"

"I just forgot to do laundry and ran out of underwear, if you must know," Cash replied. He'd looked all over his messy apartment just trying to find a clean uniform, and his luck had stopped there. The way things were going, he'd have to take a vacation just to catch up on laundry and dishes. That wasn't exactly his idea of fun.

Levi paused for a minute. "Did you at least throw some swim trunks on?"

Cash's frustration was building. "Nope," he retorted. "I'm going commando today. Remind me to talk to you about how rough these uniforms are, by the way. My junk is getting rubbed raw already." He slammed the handset back down on the hanger.

"I guess I'll see you in a bit. Over."

He pulled up in front of Cowpunch Coffee a few minutes later. He shouldn't have gotten snappy with

Levi. Friend or not, Levi was still his boss, and Cash was still interested in proving himself at the department. He'd have to apologize, and he was already regretting what he'd admitted over the radio. If old Doris were working dispatch that morning and heard that, she'd probably faint.

He regretted it even more when he walked inside.

The patrons all turned to look at him. This was no surprise in a small town, but then they began to clap and cheer. Several of them whistled, and a few of the older ladies were making eyes at him as he worked his way to the back corner. Cash turned around and took a bow, even though his cheeks were burning, taking it in stride before he sat down across from Levi. "You radioed me from right here, didn't you?"

Levi pointed to the handset on his shoulder. "Everyone heard you loud and clear, buddy."

"You could've told me." Cash shoved the menu aside. He'd memorized it long ago.

"That's not as much fun. Now, was it really laundry that made you late?" Levi asked. "I've noticed that's been happening with you a lot lately."

Cash ran his hand through his short, dark hair. "You know, timing was absolutely everything when I was roping. A fraction of a second made all the difference in the world. Now I'm strapped down with all this endless paperwork, or a suspect who won't shut up, or someone who swears they witnessed something incredible when nothing happened at all. I swear it's carrying over into the rest of my life, too."

"And that's why you're out of clean boxers?" Levi asked with a small smile.

"Again, you could've told me you were already in here and not in your cruiser," Cash noted.

Levi shrugged. "Everyone will know who you are. That's one way to make a name for yourself."

"Thanks a lot."

"Hey, you're Wade's best friend. We all grew up together. You can't ask me to give you any preferential treatment, right?"

Levi had been messing around, but that struck a nerve with him. If he ever got himself a promotion or a raise, Cash didn't want anyone to think it had to do with nepotism. He was stopped from explaining all this to Levi by the arrival of their waitress.

He was struck completely dumb as he watched her approach. Cash had lived in Sheridan his whole life. He'd been coming to that diner forever and knew all the waitresses, but he'd never seen this one before. His inner wolf pawed at his chest as he took in her high cheekbones and heart-shaped face. The top half of her wavy hair had been pulled back to her crown, but it fell in waves of gold and wheat down her back. The tag pinned to her apron said her name was Shiloh. The word echoed and expanded in his head, making him want an excuse to say it out loud.

"Are you guys ready to order? I can give you more time if you need it. I heard you've had kind of a *rough* day." The waitress gave Cash a wink as she held her pen poised over her pad.

Shit. Cash could take being called out on his lack of underwear in front of just about anyone in town, but this woman didn't feel like just anyone. He'd already rolled with the joke once, so he might as well do it again. "I'm sure you can smooth things out for me. I'll take a cup of coffee and a sausage biscuit."

Shiloh cocked her head at him. Her smile lit up the room, showing all of her perfectly white teeth. "You sure? It may be my first day here, but I always thought cops wanted doughnuts."

Levi snorted behind his hand.

Cash ignored him. "Did they train you to be a ball buster, or was that already on your resume?" he shot back.

Shiloh giggled as she jotted his order onto a pad.

It was a beautiful sound, one that rattled through his ears and filled his chest. "Well, I hope you don't mind, because I'm not changing anytime soon. You're just gonna have to get used to me."

Levi cleared his throat. "I'll have the number three, please."

"Sure thing. I'll have it out right away." Shiloh gave another wink before she moved back toward the kitchen.

Cash watched her walk away. He wasn't sure he'd ever get used to a woman who could make him feel like that, but he didn't mind a bit.

There were plenty of beautiful women in Sheridan, both the locals and the streams of tourists that came through every year. He'd seen his share while on the road with the rodeo circuit, too; enough that he didn't think of himself as a sucker for a pretty face or a nice smile. They were one in a million, right? But he sure didn't mind the way she looked when she walked away, even in that stiff cotton waitressing dress that looked like it'd been around since the fifties.

"Earth to Cash," Levi muttered.

"Sorry." His face flushed as he realized he'd been caught staring, and he ran a hand through his dark hair. "Anyway."

"Anyway," Levi continued for him, looking serious as hell. "We've got to talk about the Stanton case from last week."

Well, shit. It was one thing to get called out for staring at a cute waitress, but this was far more embarrassing. "Do we really have to keep talking about this? I said I was sorry."

Levi shook his head, looking disappointed. "We do, because I'm in charge of the whole county's safety. I can't have my deputy interviewing a potential suspect and showing them all our cards. We were lucky that we still managed to get him behind bars."

Cash sighed. Stanton had been accused of drug trafficking, and it was important that they get as much information out of him as possible. Cash had zeroed in on that with laser focus, sure that this would be the case that would prove to Levi and the other deputies that he wasn't just some cowboy who got lucky enough to get a job at the sheriff's department. Unfortunately, he'd lost track of himself. Every time Stanton had denied something or said he couldn't remember who he'd sold to or bought from, Cash had presented him with the evidence they had that he was lying. "Look, I didn't mean to show them all our cards. I was just determined to get all the information out of him, and he was pissing me off."

"I understand that, but you've got to have more control," Levi cautioned. "You're going to find plenty of people in this job that piss you off. Stanton wasn't some teenager that you could scare into confessing, or at least not that way."

"Yeah, I know. Turns out it was a lot easier working with horses than people," Cash grumbled. He missed his rodeo days. Even with all the endless practice, taking run after run until he'd had it down as perfect as he possibly could, there was something incredibly satisfying about lining up in the box, waiting for the nod, and taking off like a bat out of hell after a calf. He'd competed in a few other events as well, but roping had always been his passion. His elbow rang with pain, reminding him that he'd have to find a new one.

Levi smiled sympathetically at that comment. "Sure. People can be the worst kind of animals. I'm not going to completely blame you for this one. I shouldn't have sent you in without giving you a little more training. Next time, we'll conduct the interview together."

"Right." In a way, this was Levi being nice. He was trying to take some accountability for the goof-up, and Cash knew he didn't have to do that. But if Levi had to come along and hold his hand, then he was just going to catch hell from all the other deputies. Again. "You don't have to do that."

Levi leveled a serious look at him, one that brooked no argument. "Yes, I do."

Shiloh returned just then. She bent over the table to set a mug in front of each of them and poured a hot serving of coffee. A bit of it dribbled on the table, and she whipped a napkin out of her apron pocket to mop it up. The napkin was already stained with coffee, indicating she'd been having this trouble all morning. It didn't seem to bother her, though, and Cash had to admire that.

"You said it's your first day?" he asked, just looking for some sort of excuse to talk to her. He still wanted to find a reason to say her name, to feel the way it would roll off his tongue.

She gave him another smile and a little shrug of her shoulder that sent another slosh of coffee out of the carafe and onto the floor. "Yeah, but at least I didn't pour it in your lap. I'll be back with your food."

"Sure thing."

Levi rubbed his top lip. "Don't get yourself too distracted, Cash. When I hired you, you told me all about how you wanted to climb up through the ranks, how you were determined to be the best damn deputy in the county. I don't have any doubts that you can do this, but I can promise you it's not going to happen nearly as fast if you go running off after a woman."

Cash thought seriously about teasing Levi over the new mate in his life, the woman the sheriff had met online and brought into his home, only to find that she was running from some serious problems. The rumors about it had spread among the shifters in the community, even outside of Levi's bear clan, but not in a bad way. Cassidy had been accepted, and Cash knew he could step over the line far too easily. "Yeah. I get it."

But when they were done eating and Levi had taken off quickly to take a phone call from his son, Cash found himself striding over to the counter. Shiloh was behind it, humming to herself as she clumsily cut a piece of pie for a customer who wanted dessert with their breakfast. "Oh, hi! Did you need something else?" she asked as she licked a bit of apple filling off her thumb.

His throat tightened as he watched the tip of her tongue slip over her flesh. Why was this woman so damn attractive? Sure, she was cute, but this was different. His inner wolf was howling inside him like his life depended on the question he was about to ask. "Just to know if you're free on Saturday night."

"Oh." Shiloh tipped her head up as though she were thinking, but then she blinked as she realized what he was actually asking. "Oh! I'll get off here at seven."

"I'll pick you up right after work, then."

A serious look came over her face as her brows lowered and her jaw tightened. She leaned against the counter, getting so close to him that he could feel beads of sweat threatening to boil out of his forehead. "Can you do me a favor?" she whispered.

His mouth and throat were as dry as a desert. "Sure," he rasped.

"Wear some boxers," she replied, patting him on the arm. "It's the gentlemanly thing to do, I'm sure."

"Aw, hell. I'll see you Saturday." Cash turned around and left before she could give him any more of a hard time, but now he couldn't wait to get through the rest of the workweek.

2

"Well, here it is." The landlord, Mr. Fulton, flopped his hand toward the apartment with very little enthusiasm. "I haven't had a chance to repaint since the last tenant, but you did say you wanted something right away."

Shiloh stepped inside. The place was small, even smaller than the mountain cabin she was used to living in, but it sent a thrill of excitement spiraling up through her stomach and into her throat. Mr. Fulton was right. The place definitely did need a paint job. The light fixture had a collection of cobwebs. She could tell the carpet had been cleaned based on the humid smell of shampoo in the air, but it was the most hideous brown shag carpeting she'd ever seen. There was a bedroom through one door and a bathroom through another, with the kitchen occupying a corner of the living room. "I'll take it."

Mr. Fulton frowned at her. "Aren't you even going to ask about the deposit and the rent? Or the laundry facilities?"

"Oh, right. Please tell me about all that." She folded her hands in front of her as she slowly walked around the place, peeking out the window at the street below and listening to the thump of a radio somewhere else in the building.

"First and last month's rent for deposit. No pets. If you feel like painting, I might give you a discount on the rent for doing it yourself. I'll come and look at it, though, so don't think you can trick me on that," he warned. "Laundry is in the basement. And if something breaks, call me during business hours."

"Sure. Of course." Some of that was going straight over Shiloh's head, but she'd just have to figure it all out later. She wasn't about to tell him this was her very first time renting an apartment or living on her own. Shiloh was pretty sure he wasn't going to care, anyway.

"All right. I'll go get the paperwork from the office." He turned and headed down the hallway.

Shiloh bit her lip, but she couldn't stop the grin that spread over her face. The last few months had been hard. She missed her Aunt Adelaide terribly and would have given anything to have her back. On the other hand, this was the first time she'd had a chance to make all her own decisions, to truly be on her own. She didn't hear Mr. Fulton's tired, heavy steps returning just yet, and she took the chance to fling out her arms and spin through the middle of the living room.

"First apartment on your own?" a voice asked from the door.

Shiloh nearly tripped over her own feet as she stumbled to a stop and looked up. A woman about her age with short dark hair was leaning against the doorway. A long chain hung from one ear and a stud was stuck in the other. Her crop top showed off her flat stomach, and her jeans were more holes than they were denim. Aunt Adelaide wouldn't have approved of this girl at all, yet Shiloh found that she liked her instantly. "Is it that obvious?"

"You look like Julie Andrews in *The Sound of Music*," the woman laughed, her eyes crinkling at the corners, "but I like it. My name is Alexis. I live next door."

"It's nice to meet you." Shiloh darted forward with her hand out, but the slightly stunned look from Alexis had her trying to figure out what to do with it. She stuck it in the pocket of her uniform, instead. "I was living up in the mountains, but I got a job at Cowpunch Coffee, and the drive was getting to be too much."

Alexis twisted her face, giving Shiloh a quizzical look. "In the mountains? Holy shit, that's a hell of a commute for a waitressing job. You must've been desperate to get away, huh?"

"Um." Shiloh could still hear Aunt Adelaide in the back of her mind, telling her how few people they could trust and that it was never a good idea to give away too much about herself. She instantly liked Alexis, which made it hard. "Yeah. Something like that."

Her new neighbor still had that look on her face, and it suggested that she either didn't quite believe Shiloh or she knew there was more to the story. Shiloh was fairly certain Alexis didn't have a clue, but she'd have to leave it that way for now. "Anyway, I'm just one door down if you need anything. I work a lot, but I like to party a lot, too. We'll have to go out sometime."

"Yeah, that would be great!"

Alexis gave Shiloh a smile and a wave before heading back to her place, where the thumping of music started up again.

Shiloh braced her hands on the windowsill. She picked them back up and brushed the dust off her palms before she peered down at the town of Sheridan again. Her life had changed so much in just the last couple of weeks. She spared a thought for Aunt Adelaide and was instantly transported to their little cabin up in the rugged wilderness of the Big Horns.

"There you go." Aunt Adelaide bobbed her head, making the small gold key she always wore around her neck shift against her homemade dress. "Just keep going like that. You've got the scales down pat, but now you've got to work on your wings."

"But it hurts!" Shiloh stood in the front yard in a sundress, something that wouldn't tear if she managed to get her wings to come out. Not that she was going to make it happen. No matter how hard she tried, no matter how much coaching she got from her aunt, her back remained smooth. "Maybe I'm not really a dragon at all. Maybe I'm a snake or something."

Adelaide clucked her tongue, but she also let out a little laugh. She clutched the key around her neck as she walked closer to her niece. "Trust me, child, you're very much a dragon. If you were a snake, then it wouldn't hurt at all. You wouldn't have those wings just dying to come out."

Shiloh stuck her chin out. "Maybe I'm just a really bad dragon."

"Fine. I'll make you a deal. I'll push you off the ridge. If your wings don't come out, then I'll agree that you're a snake and I'll never ask you to summon your wings again." Adelaide gave her a challenging stare.

"But..." Shiloh had spent plenty of time exploring their section of the mountains, going as far as Adelaide allowed and then as far past that as she dared when she thought her aunt wasn't looking. "It's steep! I'll die!"

Adelaide put her hands in the air. "If you don't want to do it, that's fine. Just don't say I didn't give you a way out of this."

Sighing in frustration, Shiloh knew she'd better give it another shot. Despite all the encouragement Adelaide had given her, she just couldn't find all of her inner dragon. Shiloh could feel it inside her. She knew it was there. She just couldn't get it to show itself on command. There was no way out of this, though, and so she tried again.

Shiloh closed her eyes and felt the dragon stir. It was hot as the flames that she was told she could produce one day. That heat had scared her at first, but Shiloh had learned to accept it as a welcome contrast to the cool rocks and trees that surrounded her. With her skin already transformed into an armor of dark gold scales, the rest of this shouldn't be hard. It should be right there, ready to come out. Shiloh pulled in a deep breath and let it out slowly as she envisioned her wings.

Pain ripped through her back and spread throughout her body. She screamed as she fell to her knees and then forward on her hands, gripping the earth beneath her as she looked for some solace. Tears leaked from the corners of her eyes, and she let out a great, heaving sob. "I can't do it," Shiloh wept.

"My darling." Adelaide was on her knees in front of Shiloh, and her cool hand brushed the tears from her niece's scaled face. "You did it. Your wings are beautiful."

SHE'D LEARNED SO MUCH FROM AUNT ADELAIDE, who'd worked so hard to instill in her everything she needed to know about being a dragoness. Shiloh was the last of her line now that Adelaide was gone, yet it was clear from the encounters she'd been having in Sheridan that she still had so much to learn. These lessons weren't about what it meant to be a dragon or which berries were safe to eat, but about how to live in a town among other people. Alexis clearly knew exactly what she was doing. Mr. Fulton knew enough about it that it'd already bored him to tears. And then there was Cash.

He'd struck her from the moment he'd walked into the restaurant. In that lingering moment before all the laughter of the other patrons had told her he was the guy on the radio with no underwear on, Shiloh had felt time freeze. She'd wanted to slip between the tables and cut past the old man in the corner who said she still owed him a cup of coffee, to come up in front of Cash and just look at that handsome face a little closer. She'd gotten a bit of a look at him when she'd had to take his order and bring him his food, but Shiloh had felt his gaze right back on her. Somehow, that made it so much harder.

It already felt like everyone was staring at her as she tried to learn the ropes of her first-ever job. Her new boss, Barb, had made several remarks, asking her if she'd ever seen a dishwasher before and muttering under her breath, but she was kind enough about it. Then there was just the sheer number of people who came in and out of the diner, and they all fascinated her. She'd only been used to the company of one person, and more than once, she'd had to remind herself to stop staring. Shiloh could handle that, but then of course, she'd had to slop the coffee on the table in front of Cash.

That coffee was the same color as his eyes, and she'd felt her skin sing as those eyes had whisked over her body and back to her face again. He made her grin like an idiot, even more than the new apartment did. Barb had warned her that some men around there were still a bit old-fashioned, that they thought it was all right to pinch the waitresses' butts or leer down their necklines, but this hadn't been like that at all. Shiloh didn't know how to describe it, except that nervousness and excitement clashed for space in her chest as she thought about her first real date.

"Here we go." Mr. Fulton came back into the apartment, waving a piece of paper that looked like it'd been stepped on. "We'll get this done, and I'll give you a key as soon as I get your deposit."

Shiloh pulled a pen out of her pocket. "Where do I sign?"

3

Cash felt his stomach fold in on itself as he pulled up in front of Cowpunch Coffee. He'd never been nervous about going to this old diner before, only hungry. He didn't even get nervous about dates, either. There was something about Shiloh that changed everything. He'd been thinking about her all week, wondering how this was going to go. He'd rehearsed a thousand conversations in his mind, preparing what he would say, yet he felt like he'd never been on a date before. He turned off the engine and cracked his knuckles, steeling himself to go inside, but the front door to the diner swung open before he even got his seatbelt unbuckled.

Shiloh came bouncing out of the restaurant, having changed into a pale pink sundress. A light brown belt cinched it in the middle and matched her wedge sandals. She'd threaded big gold hoops through her ears, and her hair was long and loose down her back. Shiloh swung open the passenger door and climbed into the seat, bringing the scent of roses wafting to Cash's nose. "Hey there."

"Um, hi," he stammered, feeling like he'd just been hit by Hurricane Shiloh and hadn't even had the foresight to take shelter. "I would've come in for you."

"Oh. Sorry." She glanced at the door handle and laughed. "Want me to go back in and we can try again?"

"No, that's all right. I just didn't want you to think I was the kind of guy who would sit outside in his truck instead of doing the polite thing." He fired up the engine. His wolf was on all fours, paying complete attention to the beauty by his side. She was all softness and flowers and happiness as far as he could tell, but he knew from the sass she'd given him at the diner previously that her bubbly nature didn't mean she was stupid. She had a sharp mind and a sharp tongue, and he liked that.

"The polite thing? You mean like wearing underwear?" she teased, proving his point as he backed out of his parking space.

Damn it. He had that one coming. "I'm all covered on that front. Anyway, do you like Dominic's?"

Shiloh had been staring out the window with interest, but now she turned her head. "Who?"

"Dominic's, the restaurant," he clarified. "I managed to get a last-minute reservation."

She crossed her arms in front of her chest and lifted an eyebrow. "I see. So I just get finished with a twelve-hour shift at a diner, and you're going to take me out to eat?"

"Shit. I'm sorry. It was just an automatic thing. I mean, going out for dinner..." He fumbled for the right words, realizing how stupid he looked for doing such a thing.

But Shiloh giggled and slapped him playfully on the arm. "I'm just messing with you. I've never eaten at Dominic's, so I couldn't say. I'm sure it's fine, and I'm starving."

"So you just like giving me hell?" he challenged as he rolled to a stop at a red light.

Her honey brown eyes were intense as she looked into his. "Is that a problem?"

"Not as long as you like getting it right back." Cash had been raised to be polite to women, and certainly his work with the sheriff's department demanded it, but once again, he could tell that Shiloh was different.

One corner of her mouth quirked up a little more than the other. "Sounds like you and I are going to get along just fine."

The waiter at Dominic's showed them to a table in the corner. Potted palms blocked them off from other diners, and a lit candle in a jar in the middle of the table cast a golden glow over Shiloh's face as Cash sat across from her. He could see the way she was staring at everything, watching both the diners and the waitstaff. "It's not too much like work for you, is it?"

"Hm? No, not at all. Actually, I was just thinking about how different it is. People come into Cowpunch Coffee because they want something quick and filling, and they don't want to pay a whole lot for it. I mean, that's how Barb summed it up, but I think she was right."

"Barb?"

"My boss," Shiloh replied without missing a beat. "Here, I see more people sitting around waiting for food than actually eating it."

"It's just not that sort of place," Cash said slowly. Had she never been to an upscale restaurant before? The pressure was really on him if he was the first guy to treat her right. "It's about the atmosphere and the service just as much as it is the food."

"I see. So the waitresses won't be spilling coffee every time they pour it. That would explain the pristine tablecloths, wouldn't it?" She grinned at her self-deprecating joke.

"Don't give yourself too hard of a time. You said you only just started. Is Cowpunch your first waitressing job?" Cash cringed when he realized he sounded like he was pointing out how many mistakes he'd seen her make.

Shiloh apparently hadn't taken it that way. "It's my first job, *period*," she said matter-of-factly.

"Really?" She had to be at least in her mid-twenties. How could she have never had a job? Was she some rich girl with a trust fund?

The waiter brought their menus and explained the specials before she could answer, but when he left and her eyes widened at the prices, Cash knew his first assumption had been wrong. "Holy shit!" Shiloh whispered, leaning over to point out the price of a steak. "I think you could buy the whole cow for this price!"

"Don't you worry about any of that."

"If you say so." She blinked and shook her head, still disbelieving.

Clearly, Shiloh was far more conservative when it came to money than most anyone he'd met before. He knew plenty of girls who would kill to be taken out to a restaurant like Dominic's. It wasn't as though Cash was rolling in the green, but he hadn't expected her to have this kind of reaction. Given what she'd said about her job, there was obviously a lot he had yet to learn about her. "So, you were saying that Cowpunch is your first job?"

Shiloh nodded. "Yeah. I know it sounds a little odd. I didn't realize that until I came into town to find a job, and all the managers wanted to know why I didn't have experience. The thing is, my parents died when I was young. They went on vacation, had an accident, and never came back. My Aunt Adelaide raised me, and as I got older, I was too busy taking care of her to do anything different. She passed away a couple of months ago, so a lot has changed for me since then." She paused and pressed her lips together. "I'm sorry. I shouldn't have said all that."

"No, that's okay. That's the whole point of what we're doing, right? Getting to know each other better?" What he didn't say was how much he liked her voice, how it sounded like some form of enchanting music that he could never get tired of listening to. Or how much he liked watching the way she rolled her hands through the air as she talked, or how she watched everything in the world around her like it was new.

"I guess so, yeah." In a suddenly shy way, she tucked a strand of hair behind her ear. "So, what about you, then? How long have you been a deputy?"

"Just a few months," he admitted. Cash could've lied about that to impress her, but Shiloh clearly wasn't like that. He found himself wanting to be his true self and not just some façade that he put on so the date would go well. It was nice, even if his wolf was still sniffing the air and trying to figure out how to get closer. Cash could be polite, but he was still an animal inside. "I used to be a team roper, and my partner and I would work the rodeo circuit every year. Someone sabotaged us last season, and I broke my arm. I was lucky enough that it healed okay, but I knew I couldn't go back to that again."

Her eyes widened and she leaned her elbows on the table, listening closely. "The rodeo? That seems like a huge change."

"It was. Is, actually. I'm still getting used to it. It feels like I had this great rhythm down when it came to roping, and now I'm just flinging myself from one side of the county to another like a ragdoll. It's been a hard adjustment, even though in general, I do like the work. I like the idea of keeping the area safe." Cash paused. Why the hell had he said all that? This was their first date, and he hardly knew her. If this had been someone else, he would've just said a bunch of bullshit about how he was single-handedly keeping all the rabble out of Sheridan and how she'd be safe with him.

Her eyes met his as though she'd sensed his hesitation, and Cash could swear he knew exactly how she'd felt when she'd been speaking about her life only a moment ago. Shiloh gave him a sweet smile. "I'm sure you do a good job. I don't know Sheriff Morgan well, not beyond what he likes for breakfast, but he seems pretty serious. He wouldn't keep you on if you didn't do a good job."

"Well, maybe." He could dive into all the politics of being best friends with the sheriff's twin brother later. She didn't have to know *everything* about him, right?

The waiter brought their meal, and they were both saved from any further awkward conversation for the moment. Shiloh joked about the chef wanting to keep all the good food to himself, and that's why the portions were so small, and Cash found himself joining right in on the fun. He was going crazy for this woman and in such a short span of time that he found himself trying to understand why. It was like there was a connection between them, like he'd already known her even before they'd met. Cash knew what an older shifter would tell him, but he'd never really thought he'd find his destined mate. That was an urban legend, the kind of thing grandmas liked to hope for, but that would never really happen. Still, it made him question the reaction that not just his human side was having, but his wolf.

"I'd like to ask you something," Cash said when their dishes had been cleared and they were waiting for a slice of decadent chocolate cake that he'd hardly paid any attention to. "It's kind of a personal question."

She dabbed the corner of her mouth with a napkin. "Well, you've already seen me completely inhale that salmon fillet, so I think we can get a little personal."

Cash gripped his tongue in his teeth for a minute as he gazed at her. It was the kind of thing that a shifter hardly ever asked another shifter. They didn't usually need to, because they already knew the answer. Still, every time his wolf reached out, it was met with something it couldn't quite identify. "What kind of shifter are you?" he asked quietly.

Shiloh had been happy to laugh off the idea of a question that was too personal, but it was clear from the look on her face that he'd managed to cross the line. Her lips parted as her eyes darted off to the side. "Does it really matter?"

"No," he replied quickly. "I just...I was curious. I can usually tell. There are a lot of shifters around Sheridan, from wolves to bears to lions. I just don't think I've met anyone like you."

"Probably not." She bit her lower lip.

Did she have any idea how hot she looked when she did that? *Stay on track, Cash.* "You don't have to answer. I didn't mean to make you uncomfortable."

"No. No, that's okay. I've just never really told anyone before." Her body shuddered with what Cash thought was a chill, but then she looked down at her hands in her lap and smiled. "It seems that my inner animal wants you to know anyway."

Cash watched in awe as she lifted her arm and set her hand on the table. Her fingertips nearly touched his near that flaming candle, and in its glow, he could see gleaming gold scales trailing down Shiloh's forearm.

"I'm a dragon," she explained softly.

4

SHILOH WATCHED THE LIGHTS OF DOWNTOWN Sheridan go by, feeling the town still held many secrets she had yet to unlock. She'd thought she was a bit of a secret herself, at least until she'd gotten herself around Cash. Shiloh had watched his face carefully as she'd shown him her scales. Adelaide would've been furious with her for doing such a thing, and Shiloh never would've entertained the idea of telling someone who was almost a complete stranger. She couldn't quite seem to help herself around him, though. Cash had taken in the scales, even taking her hand and running the tip of his finger gently over them. Then he'd merely nodded, as though he'd known all along.

"So, it really doesn't bother you that I'm a dragon?" she asked as they headed across town to her apartment.

He glanced at her before looking at the road again. The corners of his mouth were curled up slightly. "No."

"You're sure it doesn't bother you that I could just swoop down on some poor rancher's field and clean him out of his cattle in one night if I wanted to?"

Cash lifted a shoulder. "I like a girl with an appetite."

She laughed at that. "Fair enough. I'll try to behave for the time being and keep my wings tucked away."

"You don't have to do that for my sake," he said, his eyes glittering. "I don't plan on keeping my wolf hidden forever. I'll show you my teeth if you show me yours."

Her entire body was on fire. It wasn't the sort of flame that she built up inside her chest when she was in her reptile form, either. This was an inferno that rippled over her skin and echoed throughout her body every time Cash looked at her. Shiloh could swear she sensed his wolf reacting to her dragon. The logical side of her brain had no idea how to deal with this, but the more intuitive side only knew that she wanted to be as close to him as possible for as long as she could.

Before she could throw another tantalizing quip back at him, she saw her ramshackle building out of the corner of her eye. "That's my place. Want to come up for a bit?"

Cash eased his truck onto the side of the street. "That depends. Don't dragons have big fiery caves full of gold and treasures?"

He'd teased her about giving him hell, but Shiloh liked to see that he was giving it right back to her. Cash was exciting, and she felt her dragon urging her on. "Of course, but I'm sure I can find some old bones for you to chew on."

"Such hospitality is impossible to resist," Cash retorted.

Shiloh fished her keys out of her purse as they walked up the stairs. "In all reality, I just moved in the other day. I still have a lot of stuff to unpack, and it's kind of a mess, but I really like this little place."

Alexis met them coming down the hall. She waved her fingers at Shiloh and waggled her eyes suggestively at Cash. "Hey, girl. Don't worry about keeping me up tonight. I'll be out late."

Shiloh's face burned as she unlocked her door. There was still so much to navigate when it came to living in town with other people. In some ways, she thought Adelaide hadn't done her any favors by keeping her so isolated.

Cash did the same thing she'd done when she'd first checked the place out. He braced his hands on the windowsill—which had been dusted off now—and looked outside. "Nice view."

Shiloh stood back, tapping her fingernail on her teeth. Cash had looked good in his uniform when she'd seen him at Cowpunch Coffee. Now, getting a chance to see him from behind—where she wasn't distracted by those dark eyes of his—she could see that it didn't have anything to do with the uniform at all. His tight jeans hugged his backside and showed off the muscled length of his legs. Maybe it was the years he'd spent roping, but he sure didn't look like he just sat around in a squad car all day. The same could be said for the way his button-down shirt stretched across the width of his upper back and shoulders. "Yes, it really is."

He turned then, seeing that she was meaning him and not the view from the window. "You know, if you keep talking to me like that, it's only going to get harder to control myself."

Shiloh grinned at him as they drew closer to each other. Her body seemed to sense every part of him, measuring the slight distance between them and demanding that it be less. "That's kind of what I was hoping."

He had her in his arms then, his head bent as he kissed her gently at first and then more urgently. Cash's arms had closed around her, but now he slid his hands over her back, down around her waist and to her hip bones, and then pressing against her backside. It was like he couldn't quite decide where to put them, wanting them everywhere.

A thrill of energy claimed Shiloh's body as Cash's powerfully muscled arms moved around her. She felt more than heard a growl of desire in his throat as she, too, tried to satisfy her hands with only what she could touch. Shiloh wanted all of him, all at once. Her fingers glided along the bulky muscles of his biceps and coasted up to explore the edges and recesses of his shoulders and the back of his neck. She buried her fingertips in his hair, feeling their bodies melding together, welding with the heat of this newfound passion. She welcomed it, knowing this was exactly what she'd been missing in her life. The sensation of exploring his body like this was almost overwhelming, but Shiloh reveled in sensing just how badly he wanted her.

That kiss had ignited something in him, too.

Cash's fingers expertly flicked the strap of her sundress out of the way so that he could drag his full lips down the slope of her neck. A shiver of pleasure made her shimmy against him, and his breathing became more ragged as he paid the same attention to her other shoulder. "Shiloh," he breathed, her name like a spell on his tongue that made her throw the very last ounce of caution she had gleefully into the wind.

Slowly, Shiloh pulled his shirt out of the waistband of his jeans. She felt her breath quicken as she undid the buttons, feeling him watching her as she parted the fabric to touch his wide chest and the dark curls that spread across it. Peeling his shirt away, she reached for his belt buckle. Her heart leapt in her chest as she unzipped his jeans, feeling all the excitement of the evening buzzing through her.

Cash's fingers were nimble and warm as he peeled away the bodice of her dress. It wasn't the sort of garment that allowed for a bra, and he groaned when he saw her bare breasts underneath. He dipped his head and pulled one into his mouth as he stripped the rest of her dress away, leaving it as a puddle of pink fabric on the floor.

With his naked body pressed against hers, Shiloh couldn't remember a time when she'd felt more free. The feeling of his skin against hers, his mouth grazing her body, and her growing surge toward him was a heady mixture that she felt in the marrow of her bones. Shiloh lifted a leg and wrapped it around him, feeling his hardness pressing urgently against her.

The two of them stumbled together into the bedroom, both of them knowing what they wanted and neither willing to let go of each other on their way there. Shiloh felt a quiver shudder through her body as they tumbled onto the bed, set up only yesterday and covered in crisp white sheets. She held him tightly and gasped as he entered her, his member thrusting its way toward her deepest secrets.

Shiloh closed her eyes and focused on the way their bodies fit together as he moved inside her. She pressed her cheek to his shoulder and wrapped her legs around him, feeling the nuances of every thrust, but there was something more. Her dragon was more alive than she'd ever felt it. It swirled inside her, but it also reached outside her body. Shiloh gasped as she felt it connecting with Cash's wolf, the two animal spirits fastening to each other as their human counterparts found their connection.

It was incredible. Her body was melting as she

felt him inside her, yet Shiloh knew she wanted more. She whipped one leg down and pushed him off of her. Cash registered surprise for only a moment before he understood what she wanted, and he grabbed her by the waist as he rolled over onto his back. As she sank down around him once again, he ran his hands up her ribcage as though he were sculpting it from clay, holding and tracing every line. His thumbs mapped the planes of her stomach, and his tongue flicked the hard buds of her nipples as she rode him.

Shiloh tipped her head back, her entire body alight with desire. She never wanted this to end, yet she wanted so desperately to get to that final culmination that would bring her ultimate satisfaction. She dug her knees into the mattress on either side of Cash and thrust her hips down until she felt him inciting a riot of spasms within her. His grip on her hips tightened, and she could feel his cock engorging even more. Tension built like a bubble within her until it finally let go, and she cried out as she felt it release. Cash's breath came in staggered gasps as he let himself go, his fingers digging into her backside as his climax met hers.

5

It was a bright and sunny day as Cash went on patrol, threading through Sheridan's streets and outer roads, but he didn't see any of it. Even behind the wheel, the only thing he could see was Shiloh twisted in those stark white sheets, the pale fabric gracing her beautiful naked body, showing just enough of her curves and hinting at the rest of them.

There hadn't been any discussion about whether or not he would stay the night, but he hadn't been interested in leaving, and she hadn't made any mention of kicking him out. He'd spent the remaining night hours with her pulled up against him, wrapped in his arms, the spun gold waves of her hair splayed over his shoulder. He'd woken up several times, thinking he was having some incredible dream. Every time he discovered that his fantasy was a reality, he drifted back off into a deep sleep.

It had been incredibly hard to leave the next morning, but now the wait was even harder. He couldn't just call her. Could he? The rules were that you waited a few days. Somewhere in the back of his mind, Cash knew there was supposed to be some sort of reason or logic behind that, but he sure as hell couldn't find it now. He tapped the steering wheel, seriously considering leaving his patrol route and heading back to Cowpunch Coffee just for the chance to see her again. He really didn't care if he was supposed to be making her wonder if he wanted to see her. Cash knew he definitely did.

"Cash, it's Levi." The sheriff's voice crackled over the radio.

Shit. That couldn't be good. If dispatch had something for him, they would've thrown it out over the air in code and sent him on his way. Cash picked up the handset and held down the button. "Cash here."

"I need you to get to the station. I've got to talk to you."

"Be there in a few." Cash hung the handset back up and spun around to head back to the station, cursing himself the entire way. What the hell had he done now?

Eve was sitting at her desk in the front office. She was a sweet woman who treated all the deputies like family, and she always made little goodie bags for their children during the holidays. Cash had taken to her quickly. He saw her purse her lips as he walked through the door, though, and he knew that couldn't be a good sign. "He's in his office," she said quietly.

"Thanks." Cash passed Eve's desk and threaded through the department to the one office that actually had a door on it.

Levi was sitting behind his desk, staring grumpily at his computer screen. He looked up at Cash when he entered and gestured with his hand. "Shut the door."

Double shit. Cash did as he was told and decided to head off the reprimand at the pass. "Look, if this is about me being late this morning—"

"Actually, being late is about the only thing you're doing consistently." Levi leaned forward and tapped his fingers on the desk thoughtfully. "Just a few days ago, I was reprimanding you for diving in too deep on a case and getting in over your head. Now, it sure looks to me like you're going to the complete opposite end of the spectrum and slacking off. Your paperwork is hardly even filled in." He produced a folder from a drawer and slapped it onto the desk.

"I, um, I guess I've just been a little distracted." Cash scratched the back of his head. He hadn't thought about it until now, but he'd been so busy thinking about Shiloh that everything else had fallen to the wayside. Her beautiful hair, those dazzling eyes, the way her skin felt under his fingers...

"You're going to find plenty that could distract you from this line of work," Levi said sternly. "We all have private lives. We all have our other concerns. But when you're on the clock, you damned well better be paying attention to what you're doing. This isn't the kind of place where mistakes can be easily fixed, especially when they can create life-or-death situations. Clear?"

"Yes, sir." Cash hated this part of his job. He liked Levi, but it was hard to report to someone. He was used to being his own boss. If he failed his run during a rodeo, then he only had himself to blame. Even though he knew he was still very much at fault for the mistakes Levi was talking about, he'd much rather chastise himself than hear it from someone else.

"Now, if you don't think you're too distracted to handle it, I've got a call I'd like you to check out. There are some campers up near the mountains, and I'm getting reports that they're on land where camping isn't allowed. I don't know why the hell anyone would do that since there are plenty of places to pull in legally, but I learned a long time ago that things don't always make sense in this line of work. They must be loud or obnoxious in some way, or else I doubt the other campers and tourists would really care. Go check it out for me."

"Sure thing." Cash got the information from Levi on the location and left. He nodded to Eve, who was watching him with worried eyes, and headed out to his squad car. This call was just a waste of time, and he knew it. It was an underhanded punishment from Levi for not doing his job, but at least it wouldn't be on Cash's record. It was the sort of call that no one else would want to go out on, yet Cash knew he didn't have a choice.

He felt the distance between himself and wherever in town Shiloh might be as he headed toward the mountains. Cash wondered if she was still thinking about him. She was a funny, quirky girl who was smart and sassy while still a bit naïve. He was fairly certain there just weren't other women in the world like that. His lips craved her, and he desperately wanted to feel that warm, soft body pressed against his again.

At the same time, he couldn't deny the non-physical connection he had to her. Cash could swear he'd reached out and experienced that inner dragon, a beast inside her that was just as wild and mysterious as she was. He'd only gotten to experience that proximity to it for a short time, but now he yearned for it just as much as he did her body and her smile. Cash rattled his thumb and finger against the steering wheel impatiently. He pulled over and sent her a text message.

You free tonight?

That was at least a start, and even if she was at work and couldn't text him back for a few hours, the message would still be waiting for her when she was available. Feeling a little better, Cash took 335 out toward Little Goose Peak.

It wasn't hard to find the campsite in question with the information he'd been given. Someone had pulled a couple of small RVs into the woods further up into the mountains than the official campsite.

Cash swung his cruiser over into a swath of weeds and got out.

A slim man in black jeans and a baseball cap stepped out of one of the campers. He stiffened slightly when he saw Cash, but then he lifted his hand and waved. "Hey there, deputy! What brings you out here?"

"I could say the same, considering how rough most of these roads are back here," Cash replied as he slowly approached. The RV's were small pull-behinds, and they looked to be older ones that'd been well-used. The firepit the campers had set up in the clearing had been put out appropriately, and Cash didn't notice any stray beer bottles or cigarette butts. "I'm surprised you could get those campers this far up here."

"Oh, these old things are rock solid." The man slapped the side of his camper like it was a horse. "We've had them all over the country."

Bracing his hands on his hips, Cash continued to look around. If this little campsite could be picked up and placed just a little further down the foothills, there wouldn't have been a darn thing wrong with it. So why did he feel like there was something here he was missing? "That's good. It's always nice to get out and get some fresh air. But listen, this area isn't actually cleared for camping. You're going to have to pack it back downhill."

The slim man's head bobbled back on his neck as though this were the first he'd ever heard of this news. He brushed his hand through his thick, dark stubble and adjusted the brim of his cap. "You're not really going to make us move all this, are you? I mean, we've already spent all this time getting it set up, and this gives us a great start on the trails that lead up into the prettiest parts of this country."

He was doing a decent job of pretending to be innocent, but Cash could see in his cold, green eyes that he absolutely knew he wasn't supposed to be there. It wasn't the first time since he'd come to work for the sheriff's department that he'd encountered this reaction from people. They seemed to think that acting innocent would make them so. "I'm afraid so. You'll have to start at the bottom just like everybody else. Mind if I have your name?"

The man was still standing close to his camper. He scratched his arm, and Cash noticed the large, medieval crossbow tattooed there. His other forearm bore several symbols, but Cash didn't recognize any of them. "Why? Are you going to write me a ticket?"

Cash lifted a shoulder and let it fall. "I don't see much point in that. If you're going to move your site, then there's no harm done. I just have to get all my paperwork done right so my boss will stay off my ass. You know how it is."

"Sure. Right. Isaiah Garrett." He held out his hand, prompting Cash to come further into the campsite to shake it.

Cash didn't like that idea. He was a deputy alone, and it was obvious from the way this site was set up that there were far more people staying there. He liked it even less when his hand touched Isaiah's, but he controlled himself well enough that the hackles of fur threatening to erupt didn't show. "Cash Taylor. Where's the rest of your crew?"

"Oh, out for a hike. I would've gone with them, but I had some food on the road yesterday that didn't agree with me. Figured it'd be safer to stay here."

"Right. Well, I'll let you get started on packing up. Just check in at the campground down below, and they can get you set up with a spot. Thanks for your cooperation, Mr. Garrett." Cash turned and headed back to his squad car, but he could feel Isaiah's stare like lasers on the back of his neck.

He made it back into the driver's seat and had to get into the weeds a bit to turn around before he headed back toward town. Cash didn't like this

Isaiah Garrett character. Not in the slightest. He waited until he was on an easier stretch of road before he radioed back to the station. "This is Taylor. I checked on the campers and I'm headed out of the mountains."

"This is dispatch. Please hold."

Cash frowned at the radio. What a strange day this was turning out to be. What the hell would they ask him to hold for? Was something going on at the department?

But a moment later, Levi's voice came through. "Got it all taken care of, Cash?"

He could see what this was all about now. Levi just wanted to give him hell. Well, that was fine. The rest of the deputies would probably do the same once they found out he'd been sent out on a wild goose chase. "Sure did. Sent them back down the mountain."

"I knew I could count on you for the job, Cash." It was Levi's cryptic way of letting Cash know that he'd served his sentence and now they could move on, at least as long as Cash behaved himself.

"Sure thing."

They signed off, and Cash stared at the long road ahead as his mind wandered back up into the mountains. Isaiah Garrett hadn't done anything more than set up his camp in the wrong spot. If he was doing anything illegal like poaching, then Cash didn't have the evidence for it nor the warrant to find that evidence. Cash had done his job, yet he had a terrible feeling there was much more going on at that campsite than he'd ever find out about. He knew how Levi felt about gut feelings, though, so he simply drove back into town.

6

Shiloh sat at the bar of the Full Moon Saloon. She took a long sip of her beer as she looked around, trying to soak it all in. The place was packed, and she couldn't remember ever seeing so many people in one place at the same time. "So these people are really...like us?" she asked Alexis as quietly as she could.

Alexis nodded and signaled the bartender for another beer. She'd already sucked down the first one like it was water. The man was tall and slim, but he had broad shoulders. His dark hair was long and pulled into a braid, making his Native American descent all the more obvious. The most startling thing about him, though, was the long scar down one side of his face that gave him a permanent scowl. He passed the beer to Alexis, gave Shiloh a long and studied look, and then headed off to take care of another client.

"Most of them, anyway," Alexis explained once he was gone. "Take Shaw, for instance. He runs this place and leads his pack. He might look scary, but he's a good egg. If any guy gives you a hard time, he'll kick their ass. But there are all sorts in here, really. Sure, a few tourists manage to wander in every now and then, but I think they tend to sense the thick, animal presence and mosey on down to someplace a little tamer."

"That's so funny. I grew up thinking that shifters were so rare, and I'd be lucky to find even one other person like me once I moved to town." She laughed a little, which was either the beer or just the sheer joy she felt at finally getting the chance to start out on her own. She had an apartment, a job, and she'd even been on a hot date.

As though she'd summoned him, she felt her phone buzz in her pocket again. Shiloh took it out, but she already knew what she'd find on the screen.

Wasn't sure if my text from earlier went through. I was pretty far out.

She frowned at the device, swiped away the notification, and put her phone back in her pocket.

Alexis cocked her head to the side with curiosity, making her long earring dangle against her shoulder. "Trouble in paradise?"

"I wouldn't put it quite like that," Shiloh replied. "Is it really paradise if it's just one date?"

"It can be, at least for a short time. Did that hunk of man fail to rock your world the other night?" Alexis took another chug of her beer, but she was still watching Shiloh intently.

Shiloh blushed slightly. She wasn't sure she knew Alexis well enough to share the details of her sex life, but it wasn't as though she had anyone else to tell. "He was good. Really good, actually." She felt a simmering of excitement in her stomach as she once again thought of the night she'd spent with Cash. He'd been absolutely incredible. It was like he'd known exactly what she wanted. She'd even been pleased to see that he'd stayed the night instead of running off into the darkness once he was done with her.

"So?" Alexis prompted. "What's the problem, then?"

Shiloh shrugged. "I don't know. I guess I just don't want to get lost in some guy when I'm finally finding a life of my own. I spent a lot of time taking care of my aunt as she got older. I wouldn't change that for the world, and she did so much for me, but now I just want this to be my turn to live. Does that make sense?" She glanced around the room, seeing all this life around her and how happy everyone was as they drank and met new people. She didn't want to miss out on anything, and she knew that latching herself to Cash's side was going to mean exactly that.

"But?" Alexis hadn't known Shiloh for very long, but she seemed to have a good sense of what she was actually thinking. She was like the best friend Shiloh had always wanted growing up, someone who had an incredible sense of fashion and tons of confidence, but who was also grounded.

"But I really like him, too. I think I feel something, but I'm not sure I'm ready to feel that." Shiloh had found it impossible not to think about Cash. He was handsome, and that didn't hurt a thing. She could look at him all day. But there was a lot more there than that. Shiloh had distinctly felt something when she'd tumbled into bed with him, and it wasn't just his pure masculinity. She desired him with something more than herself. Her longing for him was potent, and that attracted her just as much as it pushed her away.

"Give yourself some time," Alexis advised. "Just because the two of you are good together doesn't mean you have to marry him. Tell him to give you some space. If there's really something clicking, then you'll find each other again."

Shiloh stared into the foam on top of her beer. She hadn't expected such a philosophical standpoint from Alexis, who seemed to do whatever struck her at the moment and damn the consequences. "You really think so?"

"I do. Come on, Shi. We're shifters. We're not like regular humans, who get all caught up in logic and finances and couples' counseling. It's not like that for us. Whoever we're supposed to be with comes to us. I think that works on more levels than just that old 'fated mate' idea. For instance, I firmly believe that you and I were meant to come into each other's lives. My best friend moved away six months ago to pursue her career, and now here you are."

"Yeah, I guess that's true," Shiloh said with a smile. "It's working out pretty well so far."

"I agree, especially because I might not have come to this bar tonight if you hadn't been with me. I might've gone to one of my other usual haunts, and then I wouldn't have spotted that fine specimen over there." She pointed to the other side of the narrow bar, where she'd made eye contact with a handsome blonde man. He had a prominent jawline and piercing blue eyes, and he was making his way toward her.

"Looks like you're going to have a good night."

"Don't think for a second that I'm leaving you," Alexis corrected. "I said I was going to bring you out for a night on the town, and that's what I'm going to do. Just give me a minute to go dance with this guy and give him my number." She slid gracefully down off her barstool and adjusted her top.

"Don't worry about it. Looks like I'll be a little busy myself." Shiloh wasn't going to stop Alexis from having a good time, anyway, but she'd just spotted a familiar face walk through the door.

"Oh, the beefcake is back for more," Alexis noted, raising one dark eyebrow. "You know where I'll be if you need me, and don't forget that Shaw is always on your side."

Shiloh noticed Cash and Shaw nod at each other as the deputy made his way over to her. He'd just gotten off work, apparently, considering he was still dressed in uniform. He smiled, but the set of his brows and jawline suggested he was less than happy. "Hey. There you are. I've been trying to get a hold of you today." He took the liberty of taking the seat Alexis had occupied only a moment ago.

"I know," she said carefully. "I've just been busy."

"I understand." Cash smiled a little, but she could see the hesitation behind it. "I had a long shift, anyway. I just really wanted to see you again."

Shiloh felt a war brewing inside her again. Alexis had given her good advice. She didn't have to make any commitments right now, and Shiloh knew she deserved the chance to figure out who she was and what she wanted. But that deep pull she had toward Cash wouldn't stop speaking to her. It whispered to her, audible despite the roaring din of the bar. It reminded her of the times they'd shared at Dominic's and her apartment, talking, laughing, touching, tasting. Her dragon coiled inside her, demanding to know why she didn't understand what was right in front of her. Meanwhile, her human side longed for the freedom that she'd never had, not when she was a child and her aunt was trying to keep her safe and secluded, and not as she got older and had the obligation of taking care of her aging guardian. Why did this have to be so hard? Was it this hard for everyone?

"That's sweet of you," she finally said, fiddling with her bracelet and trying to decide exactly how she was going to do this. "I'm sorry I didn't text you back earlier. I've just been busy, and I've been thinking a lot."

He was instantly on guard. His shoulders stiffened, and those dark eyes had grown even darker. "About what?"

Shiloh glanced around at the busy bar. This wasn't the place to have this conversation. Alexis had said she would be safe with Shaw, but Shiloh wasn't worried about her welfare around Cash. She knew—and even her dragon knew—that he wasn't one of the ones she had to worry about. "Can we step outside for a minute?"

"Of course." Cash escorted her to the door, resting his hand ever so gently on her lower back as he opened the front door of the Full Moon Saloon.

Damn it, didn't he know how hard he was making this? It would be so easy to get caught up in the exhilaration and romanticism of a potential relationship with him. He seemed like the classic good guy, the sort of hero she'd seen on those old movies Adelaide had on VHS. But Shiloh knew she had to give herself all the chances at a life of her own that she'd always wanted. She'd never forgive herself otherwise, and she'd just end up resenting Cash. That wasn't fair to him, not now and not later.

She walked a short way down the street, just far enough not to hear too much of the throbbing music and laughter from the saloon, before turning to him.

His soft eyes made her catch her breath for a moment, but she pushed her way through. "Look, I think you're a great guy."

He'd been reaching to put his hands on her hips, but he quickly dropped them to his sides. "Oh."

"I do," she insisted. "I really like you. I just need some space before I end up getting in over my head. It's something I need to do for myself. I hope you can understand that." Shiloh watched his face carefully. Most of the time, ever since she'd come down from the mountains, she'd enjoyed getting to explore her fun and sassy side as she interacted with all these new people. She hadn't realized there was a whole other aspect to relationships, and she felt like a complete bitch.

Cash looked at her. He raised his hand, looking like he was going to touch her hair or cradle her cheek, but he dropped it. Then he parted his lips to say something and closed them again. His whole body was wavering, and Shiloh had to wonder if he was fighting an internal war similar to the one she'd been struggling with. "I understand," he finally said.

"Thanks. I don't know if this is weird, but I hope we can still be friends. I mean, I'm sure I'll see you around the diner, right?" she asked hopefully.

"Right. Okay. Well, thanks for letting me know.

I'd better get going." Cash turned on his heel and headed toward the street, but then he stopped and looked back. He gestured toward her and toward the door of the saloon. "You all right?"

The sweet thing wanted to make sure she was going to get back inside okay and not just be standing out on the street. As much as she wanted to savor her newly found freedom, she still thought that was incredibly nice. "Yeah. I'm all right." Shiloh headed back in.

Her bar stool hadn't been taken, so she regained a prime spot to watch all the customers. Alexis was still with her big blonde guy, looking happy. Everyone else did, too. Why didn't she feel that way?

7

It was dark by the time Cash pulled up to the big barn outside Sheridan. The lights were on in the house, but he knew Wade would still be out in the barn. The yellow glow in the small square windows at the top of the indoor arena told him so. He let out a sigh of frustration as he got out of his truck and headed toward the door. The air was fresh and clean, and the night stars were coming out, uninhibited by streetlamps and big signs. He could feel the wilderness that crept in around the edges of every ranch, cattle farm, and horse barn, constantly reminding the residents of Wyoming that the wild places they'd carefully cultivated over the last couple of centuries could easily be reverted.

He stepped inside the door to find the welcome

sounds of horses and men. The scent of dust and horse lather was thick in the air, making him miss the old days more than he'd realized. Wade was standing in the aisleway next to the arena, brushing down a big blue roan. He rubbed Thunder's ears as he turned to the doorway. "Cash! You're actually here. I was starting to think you weren't coming."

"Yeah, well, I got busy." Cash greeted his old roping partner before ducking under the cross ties that held Thunder in place. He moved down the row of stalls that overlooked the arena to find Wilbur, who nickered softly at his owner. "Hey, old buddy. You still remember me, huh?"

"We all do," said Colton. He was a local cattle rancher who lived just down the street from Wade, and he also happened to be in Cash's pack. "I mean, we hardly see you anymore, but we know you must be busy writing tickets for horses tied to the wrong hitching post or tumbleweeds that roll into the wrong parts of town."

"Kiss my ass," Cash muttered as he led Wilbur out of his stall and brought him over to a free set of cross ties. He knew there were plenty of folks who liked to make fun of law enforcement in a rural area like theirs just because it didn't seem as though anything ever happened. Cash knew the reality of it. "How's Wilbur been doing as a teaching horse?"

"Fantastic." Wade came around to the other side of the palomino Cash used to rope from and rested his arms on the horse's strong back. "He's staying very busy and fit, and I don't think he minds at all. He's the perfect mount for everyone from kids to adults. With all the roping clinics we're running, I don't think he has a clue that you've hung up your spurs."

Cash clenched his teeth as he ran a shedding comb over the familiar hide. "Well, maybe I'll come back."

"And trade in that shiny gold star on your chest?" Colton said. "It's nice to win a belt buckle or a fat envelope of cash, but it's not exactly the same as a steady paycheck from the county. I set all my competition days aside when I was done with high school, and sometimes even the beef industry isn't lucrative enough for me."

Wade squinted at his old roping partner. "You really thinking about quitting? You seemed pretty happy to have something new to occupy your time, and it isn't as though roping and riding is all that easy on the body in the long run."

"Yeah, well neither is sitting behind a desk,"

Cash grumbled. “No offense to that brother of yours, but working for the county just might not be my cup of tea.”

“What’s happening?”

“Levi hasn’t said anything?” Cash stepped into the tack room to grab his old saddle. ‘Old’ really wasn’t the right word for it, other than the fact that he didn’t use it anymore. He’d won it in a competition several years ago, and it would cost more than he’d paid for his first truck to replace it.

Wade shook his head. “You know my brother’s not like that, especially not when it comes to work stuff.”

“Fair enough.” Cash settled the saddle onto Wilbur’s back and then shook his arm. He already had pains shooting through it.

The gesture didn’t go unnoticed. “I thought you said the doc told you roping was out of the question. It’s been months, and you’re still not healed up right. Sounds to me like the sheriff’s department is still the right place for you.”

Cash gave him a dirty look. He knew Wade was right, but that didn’t mean he wanted to hear it. “I don’t know that I’ll have a choice if things keep going the way they are. I appreciate that Levi isn’t telling you all the gossip, but I guess if I'm the one getting reprimanded, then I have a right to share."

Colton let out a low whistle as he swung up onto the back of his gelding and headed through the gate into the arena. "That must be pretty bad if the sheriff is willing to chew out his twin brother's best friend."

"Once again, kiss my ass." The thing was, Colton wasn't entirely wrong. Levi was pretty serious when it came to his job, and he'd made it clear from the start that he wasn't interested in doing anything that could even be misconstrued as nepotism. But underneath it all, people were always a little inclined to do favors for people they knew and cared about. If he was getting called out regularly, then there was something genuinely wrong with the work he was doing. "Anyway, I just finished a twelve-hour shift and still got called into Levi's office to get my ass reamed."

There was that inquisitive look from Wade again. "Reamed over what?"

Cash sighed as he slid the halter down on Wilbur's neck and put the bridle over his ears. "I fully admit that I'm late all the time. That's completely my fault, and I'm still trying to get used to working regular shifts. But first, he gets onto me for doing too much. Then he gets onto me for being distracted and doing too little. Today, he decided I'd done too much again, jumping in on calls that should've gone to other deputies on patrol. It's not my fault they don't want to work."

"With the rodeo life, it's usually full speed ahead or moseying around waiting for something to happen. We always worked hard, but there was still a lot of downtime. Sounds like you're having a hard time finding a happy medium," Wade commented.

"That pretty well sums it up," Cash agreed with a nod. "I just don't know that I can make it work."

"So what's really going on?" Wade challenged. "Don't forget that I know you, Cash, and this isn't quite adding up. You're more adaptable than that."

Cash picked at a fleck of mud on Wilbur's hide. He opened his mouth to deny that idea completely, but he knew Wade was right. The job with the department was definitely not the same as working the rodeo circuit, but it wasn't as though it were the first position he'd ever held that wasn't on horseback. He'd worked plenty of jobs before he'd decided to do rodeo full time and before he was good enough. Wade was going to get the truth out of him sooner or later, and he might as well admit it to himself along the way. "There's this girl."

"Ohhh," the other two men groaned. Colton did

it with a roll of his eyes, but Wade had a sparkle in his.

"So did you meet her?" Wade asked. "Is this the one?"

Cash ignored yet another eye roll from Colton as the rancher took off around the arena to warm up. "I thought so," he admitted. "She's gorgeous, but it wasn't just that. She's just got this soul that I can't resist. I couldn't even stand to do the macho thing and wait around for a few days before I called her again. I thought everything went well between the two of us, but I guess I fucked it up and got too eager. The next thing I knew, she was telling me she needed space."

"Not a good start," Wade admitted. "Did she say anything else? Dick too small or something?"

The fact that there was a horse in between them was the only thing that kept Cash from punching Wade in the arm. Instead, he unbuckled Wilbur's halter and let the cross ties fall into place. "No, you asshole. She's just spent her adult life taking care of her elderly aunt, and now she wants some time to find herself."

"That's what they *all* say," Colton called out as he rode by.

Wade pursed his lips. "Sometimes they do say

that, but from what little you've told me, she might be serious. You think you felt something for real between the two of you?"

Cash was leading Wilbur to the arena, but he paused to level his gaze at his best friend. "If I didn't think it was the corniest thing in the world, I'd say the Earth moved."

"You might want to take her word for it," Wade advised. "Women aren't weak little things who rely on men for everything. They want to be independent, even if they're part of a couple. It's not something I really understood until Sierra gave me a good solid lecture a few months back."

"Yeah? She's a ball buster, too?" Cash knew that Wade's mate wasn't some shrinking violet. Considering the hell Shiloh had given him when he'd walked into Cowpunch Coffee that day, she wasn't either.

"Sometimes," Wade replied with a grin. "I kind of like it, though. But anyway, this Shiloh you're dating says she wants to find herself. So let her. Maybe you can still spend some time with her while she does that if you just back off a little bit. She's only going to resent you if the two of you go off and get married and then she suddenly realizes she wants to run away with the circus instead of being hitched to a Sheridan deputy."

"Yeah. Maybe." Cash swung up into the saddle. He'd forgotten just how comfortable it was, but he knew now that his thoughts of quitting the department didn't have anything to do with his desire to go back to his old rodeo life. It would be nothing but pain and disappointment anyway, considering the state of his arm. No, he just needed to find a way to balance his work life and feelings for Shiloh against her desire to be an unfettered woman for a while.

Wade had gone to get a couple of young cattle ready to practice roping, which meant Cash had some time to just think. Being on horseback was always a good place for that. It spoke to the soul in a different way than going for a walk on his own feet or even sitting in a comfortable chair. Maybe he didn't have to get back into the rodeo scene at all if he could just be smart enough to visit Wilbur more often.

He thought about Shiloh and what her life must have been like. She'd told him about being sent to live with her aunt when she was just a little girl. Shiloh had skimmed over the beginning as though it were simply a fact of life, but any child that'd just lost their parents had to have been traumatized. And she hadn't given him all the details, but Cash could easily imagine how lonely she must have been as she grew up isolated in the mountains without other children to play with. Once Shiloh had gotten old enough that she could've flown the nest, it was Adelaide's turn to need her.

Maybe he'd been too clingy. He didn't think it was so bad to want to spend time with her, but Shiloh still had a lot of life to explore. Wade was right; he'd just have to be patient. He only wondered if he could be patient enough to accept the distance between them.

8

SHILOH HOPPED OFF THE STEPLADDER AND STOOD BACK to admire her work. She tipped her head from one side to the other. The apartment didn't exactly look like the results in the home shows she'd watched on TV, but it was a good start. The grimy trim, dusty ceiling, and shadows of former wall hangings had been transformed into shades of clean white and pale blue with the work of a paintbrush and a roller.

Setting the roller down in the tray, Shiloh grabbed a soda from the fridge and sat on the sagging sofa. Most of the furniture in Adelaide's old cabin had been ancient, handmade stuff that weighed a ton, and so much of it had been left behind. She'd brought a few things she just couldn't stand to part with, including some macrame plant hangers and a mirror with a carved frame. Everything else had come from the local thrift store, considering that was the only place within her budget, and there were still plenty of pieces she had yet to fill in. Several cardboard boxes were still stacked in the living room, but she decided it didn't make sense to tackle them until she was done painting.

It was all cheap and mismatched, and the work she'd done to put it all together sometimes felt like far more than what should've gone into the place, but Shiloh was happy. This was what she'd wanted. She'd spent so many years living only for Adelaide. Shiloh had loved her aunt endlessly, and she would've done anything for her. That had been proven by how long she'd stayed, knowing that even though her aunt had told her not to worry, Shiloh couldn't actually leave.

She got up and looked out the window. Sheridan was a town in the middle of nowhere, yet it was bustling and busy. There were so many people there. Her heart twisted a little when she thought about Cash. It hadn't been fair that she'd met him so quickly. If she'd already had a chance to experience life on her own, she might not have dismissed him so soon.

A knock on the door gratefully pulled her away from thinking how comfortable she'd been in her bed that night with his leg thrown over her. Shiloh had told Mr. Fulton she was painting that week, so he'd probably come by to make sure she hadn't picked a color that was too funky.

But she didn't recognize the man on the doorstep. He was slim, and just a bit taller than she was. His pale green eyes were a contrast to his dark hair and the charcoal stubble on his chin and cheeks. There was another man behind him, beefy with a bald head. His hooded eyes and pursed mouth made him permanently look like someone had just insulted him. "Can I help you?"

Green Eyes touched the brim of his baseball cap and grinned. "We're actually here to help *you*, ma'am. We're with maintenance."

She shook her head slightly, trying to understand. "I didn't call for any maintenance."

"You don't have to. You see, the landlord asked us to check everything over since you've just moved in. We're gonna make sure the stove is working right, check the heat and air, go over the plumbing and electrical. Things like that." Green Eyes gave her that smile again as he took a step forward, trying to come into the apartment.

Shiloh instinctively moved in front of him, keeping the door in her right hand so that he couldn't skirt around her the other way. There was something about this man that she flat-out didn't like. Shiloh couldn't have said what it was, but no one she'd met in Sheridan so far had made her feel that way. She'd seen drunks come reeling into the diner after they'd been out on a bender who made her feel more comfortable than this guy. "Mr. Fulton didn't say anything to me about that."

"Probably just a mistake, but we do need to get the work done. I wouldn't want you to be living here all by yourself and have a problem." Green Eyes hefted the small toolbox in his hands and shook it impatiently, suggesting how much work she was stopping him from doing. The big bald guy just stood there with his hands at his sides.

Her heart was thundering in her ears, and Shiloh could feel the adrenaline throbbing through her system. It made her knees weak even as her muscles longed to engage, to take her sprinting away from these men as fast as she could. She didn't want to be scared. Shiloh had never thought of herself as the type who would run away, but even her dragon was telling her that something was wrong. It swirled inside her, swaying its head from side to side as it picked up on the strange vibes these men were putting down. It told her they would only try hard if they understood just how intimidated she was. Shiloh pulled the door shut another inch. "That's very kind of you, but it'll have to wait. I'm a little busy at the moment."

He put his palm on the door and leaned forward, revealing the large medieval crossbow tattooed on his forearm. His face was far too close to hers, and he was no longer even pretending to be friendly. "It won't take long, and we've got orders to get this done." His associate took another step closer, filling the doorway with his massive presence.

Shiloh's bones trembled. Her dragon pressed at the underside of her skin, threatening to erupt in a fury of scales. She could feel heat building in her chest. The animal inside her understood what was happening, no matter how much she wanted to deny the situation. Shiloh didn't like to think that things like this actually happened to people, but her dragon insisted this was absolutely one of those things she'd seen on late-night TV, where some guy dupes a naïve young woman into gaining access to her apartment. The beast inside was ready to come out and protect her.

Biting her lip, Shiloh forced it to stay contained.

There just aren't very many people like us in the world, my dear, Aunt Adelaide's voice said in the back of her mind. *You might think we could just shift into our true forms and do anything we want. After all, we're bigger and stronger than anyone else. But that's just one of the things that people don't like about us, and it's incredibly dangerous to let anyone—and I mean anyone—know what we really are.*

She'd already broken that rule by telling Cash. He'd been different, though. Right?

A shiver raced up her spine, making her lose control for just a fraction of a second. She felt the chill of scales on the back of her neck. Shiloh blinked to keep her eyes from changing and giving her away. "I said, you'll have to wait."

Green Eyes shoved against the door. "I'm not putting up with this bullshit, lady. Let us in so we can get the job done."

There was little she could do to control it now. The dragon was rising to the surface, rearing its head back and showing its fangs. It would take only a few seconds to completely shed the human form that everyone knew as Shiloh. She would hardly fit in this small space, but it wouldn't take long to eliminate this threat in front of her. Shiloh felt it taking over, and she wasn't sure she could stop it. She wasn't even sure she wanted to.

"Hey!" Alexis's voice cut through the air of the hallway. Her heavy black boots thundered on the thin carpet as she charged forward. The big blonde guy from the bar was right behind her, looking slightly confused but concerned. "What the hell do you think you're doing?"

Green Eyes backed out of the doorway. He smirked a little when he saw Alexis, but the broad-shouldered beefcake behind her made him recoil a little. "We're just here to do some maintenance."

"Bullshit," Alexis fired back. Her finger was pointed straight at Green Eyes, and she jabbed it in the air as though it were a weapon. "You might think a new tenant is gullible enough to fall for something like that, but I've lived in this building long enough to know that Fulton is way too cheap to hire anyone."

"We're just doing our job," the man insisted.

The man Alexis had met at the Full Moon Saloon took a deep breath that made his shoulders expand, tightening the sleeves of his shirt as he looked down his nose at the intruders. Even the big bald man suddenly looked a lot smaller. "I suggest you get your asses out of here."

Green Eyes glanced up at him again and then shook his head. "Fine." He hefted his hand around his toolbox and stormed off down the hall, his silent partner right behind him.

Shiloh sagged against the doorway. She felt like she was going to pass out, not only from the adrenaline rush of fear, but from fighting so hard against her dragon. "That was weird."

Alexis looped her arm through Shiloh's. "Just some jackasses that probably saw you coming up here with boxes and furniture who figured they could take advantage of you. But really, Fulton would never actually pay someone to do any maintenance. Or even actually do any maintenance himself," she added with a wry smile.

"I didn't know exactly why, but I just didn't like those guys." Shiloh looked down the hall, but they were already gone. She hoped they wouldn't come back.

"Oh, Shiloh, this is Dan. Dan, this is Shiloh. I don't think I had a chance to introduce you guys the other night." Alexis indicated the man she had in tow, who was also glancing down the hall in the direction Green Eyes and Baldy had gone.

"That kind of shit really pisses me off. Alexis and

I were just going to get some dinner. Why don't you come with us?" he asked.

A sob rose in Shiloh's chest. Since when had she ever been the kind of woman to cry at having some man come along and rescue her? It was just the emotional roller coaster of it all. She was tempted to decline, simply because she didn't want to bust in on their date, but she caught the grateful look Alexis had shot Dan. "That would be really nice."

9

CASH HUNG UP THE RADIO FOR THE FINAL TIME THAT evening and turned for home. There weren't a lot of tourists in town, and even the permanent residents who liked to cause trouble must have decided to spend the night in. He was tired, but a deep hunger gnawed at his stomach. Cash couldn't even remember the last time he'd eaten. He'd just grabbed a cup of coffee on his last break to make sure he could get through the night, and now he was regretting it.

He regretted it even more when he remembered that he hadn't bothered to go to the grocery store that week. He'd never liked the idea of being the guy that the older women at the checkout felt sorry for as they saw his frozen TV dinners and the smallest jug of milk you could buy go rolling by on the conveyor belt. The past couple of weeks had been even harder, and he found excuses every day instead of just getting it done. His fridge held little more than a few condiments and a beer or two.

Not that he could do anything about it now, he realized as he rolled past one of the drive-thru burger joints. All the fast-food places had closed up for the night, and the grocery store wasn't open. Even if it was, Cash wasn't sure he had the energy to bother with even microwaving something. The only place that still had their lights on, the neon sign glowing like a beacon in the night, was Cowpunch Coffee.

His stomach curled in on itself as he slid into one of the parking spots available out front. Cash looked in through the windows that lined the front of the little restaurant. He saw a man in a tattered coat hunched over the counter with a piece of pie. A young couple in the front corner held hands over the table as they gazed into each other's eyes. The older woman who often ran the restaurant—Barb, if he remembered her name correctly—sat on a stool and read the paper. There was no sign of anyone else, so Cash deemed the place safe for the moment.

He slowly climbed out of his cruiser and headed

for the front door. Even in the middle of the night, the scent of fried food wafted to him before he entered the building, and it hit him fully in the face as he walked in. His stomach growled in response.

Barb nodded at him as he walked in and took a table near the back. Cash sat down, took off his hat, and rubbed his hands over his weary eyes.

"Long shift?"

He paused with his palms still over his face. That wasn't the voice of the older woman, the one with the pouf of gray hair that'd been sitting at the counter reading the paper a moment ago. It was a much more familiar one, one that hit his ears and rang through his brain like an alarm bell. His wolf stirred, alert despite how tired he was.

Cash dropped his hands to see a vision of Shiloh standing before him. She'd tamed most of her hair into a bun, but a few strands had escaped to frame her face. Her pad and pencil were held at the ready in front of her, and she gave him a curious look of concern.

"Hey." He'd avoided the place ever since Shiloh had told him she didn't want to see him anymore. He'd decided it was best to stick with what she said and give her space, even though it killed him a little more every day. He hadn't stopped thinking about her, even if he hadn't been able to see her, and he felt everything inside him surge toward her now that she stood in front of him. "I'm, um, sorry. I thought you weren't here tonight. I don't mean to bother you." He started to get up.

"No." She put out a hand to stop him. "It's okay. It's a place of business, right?"

"Right," he said hollowly. How was it even more disappointing that she was willing to look at this objectively? Perhaps because he knew he really couldn't. Cash swallowed as he looked up at her. Something had changed about her, but he couldn't put his finger on it. "In that case, I'll just take the turkey melt and some fries."

Shiloh nodded and scribbled his order down for the cook. "Anything to drink?"

"Oh. Um, a Coke, I guess."

"I'll get that right out for you."

He watched as she walked away, but he didn't feel that same thrill of excitement he'd experienced the first time he'd seen her there. She'd been new and different, but she'd also had this energy about her that radiated out in waves and pulled him in. There'd been a light in her eyes and a spring in her step. Even the sharpness of her tongue had made him sit up and pay attention.

Was it that he'd changed, or that she had? Cash had tried to deny it as best he could, but he knew there was a hole in his heart where Shiloh had been not so long ago. It was ridiculous that a woman he'd only been on one official date with should affect him that way, yet it had. Cash had been reduced to a hollowed-out shell.

Still, he couldn't help but notice that something was different about her as well. She brought his Coke, and as he looked up at her, he saw her eyelashes brushing the hollows under her eyes. Her shoulders sagged, and she dragged herself back to the kitchen instead of springing away like a gazelle. Questions filled his mind. Had something happened? Had she searched for herself and not been satisfied with the results? It was hard to imagine that could be the case, and it disturbed him. Cash wouldn't dare imagine that it was simply that she'd missed him, that she'd realized the same thing he had and didn't know how to live without her mate.

He was trying to figure out how he was going to ask her without butting into her business when she brought out his sandwich. Shiloh placed the platter in front of him, her fingers lingering on the edge of it for just a fraction of a second. She turned back to the kitchen, but she stopped before she'd gotten more than a foot away from the table. Shiloh clutched her hands together in front of her, pausing for a long moment.

Cash felt her tension in the air. She'd completely frozen time for him, and he hadn't even managed to pick up his fork. Without saying a word, she'd put him on the edge of a cliff, waiting to see if he would fly or fall.

Shiloh spun on her heel. The next thing he knew, she was sitting in the booth across from him. Her eyes were wide and hollow as she looked at him, which only made him worry all the more. "Can I talk to you for a second?"

"Sure." He picked up his fork now, wanting something to do so he wouldn't just be staring at her. Cash didn't want to look too desperate. That was the game he was supposed to be playing, after all. "I'm not doing anything."

She flicked her lip with the tip of her tongue. "I wonder if you'd do me a favor and go with me to my cabin up in the mountains."

This made him sit back slightly and set his sandwich back down. His wolf was really paying attention now, hearing such a bold invitation from the woman who just a couple of weeks ago had claimed she didn't want to see him anymore. Cash felt a bit of a smirk creeping in at the corner of his mouth as he realized that keeping his distance might have worked. He'd just been too bold and too demanding in the beginning, and now it was paying off. "A favor? I didn't think you were interested, but I'm sure I could clear my schedule."

Her eyes flickered slightly. She'd had her eyebrows scrunched up, but now they lowered as she brought her fingers to her mouth. "Oh. Oh, no. I didn't mean like that. I'm sorry. You see, it's just that I need to get some things out of the cabin. I've been trying to get settled into my new apartment. At first, I just brought what would fit in my car. There are still a few things I'd like to have, though."

Cash picked the sandwich up once again and took a big bite. He couldn't say anything else stupid if his mouth was full, and he'd already made enough of a fool of himself. Of course she didn't want to spend a romantic weekend in a mountain cabin with him. She didn't need him the same way he needed her. But then why did she need him at all? "Can I ask you a question?" he said when he'd swallowed.

She nodded.

"You lived in this place by yourself. You've made the drive plenty of times. Why do you want me to go with you? Just to lift furniture or something?" Cash felt the spite on his tongue, but he wasn't sure he cared. That was the only reason he could see for Shiloh wanting him to come along. He was just some dumb guy who would do anything for her because he couldn't resist her. Shiloh was a smart woman, and she would've seen that. It only made him feel all the more like an idiot because he knew he'd probably do it, even if she came right out and told him that was the case.

But Shiloh shook her head as she wrapped her arms around herself. "No. There's no way I want to get that old heavy stuff up the stairs at my new place. I just have some sentimental things, some decorative objects, things like that. And..." She hesitated, looking off to the side and studying the floor.

Something was seriously wrong. The Shiloh that he'd known had been strong and bold. He would've guessed that she wouldn't be afraid of anything, considering that she'd come down out of the mountains and so fully longed to embrace the world of living in town with other people. She hadn't hesitated a second when a deputy she'd never met had asked her out, and she'd practically dragged him into bed—not that he was resisting. This was a shell of that woman, or perhaps a different one entirely.

The fire and the light that he'd found so attractive in her had diminished. "What's wrong?"

She pulled in a breath, pressed her lips together, and lifted her chin in the air, summoning some of that determination she'd always had. "I've just had some things happen recently that make me feel a little strange about going by myself. I just don't feel safe making that long drive to what's essentially an abandoned cabin alone. Aunt Adelaide always insisted that we keep the cabin a secret, and I can't take just anyone."

It had taken a lot for her to say that, he could tell. Cash took another bite of his sandwich, wanting time to think. His wolf insisted on focusing on the possibilities of being alone in the mountains with a beautiful woman—not just any beautiful woman, but one whom his soul had known since the beginning of time. The fantasies that could come out of that could keep him awake at night for a week or more.

That wasn't the point right now, though. Was he a big enough sucker that he was going to waste an entire day off work to head up into the mountains, just for her to load up her trunk with books and knickknacks? Yes. He was. He could question her why she wouldn't take her friend Alexis, but that wasn't his business. She'd asked him. That was the part that mattered. "I can do that."

"Really?" A bit of that light returned to her eyes, making a bolt of electricity shoot through his body. "I really appreciate it, Cash. Give me a call and we'll figure out a good day to do it." She hopped up from the booth bench, seemingly full of that familiar energy once again.

"Sure." Cash dug into the rest of his food, frowning down at his plate as he contemplated what he'd just agreed to. What the hell was wrong with him? He'd be willing to bet that if he asked any of his friends, they'd agree that he was being taken advantage of. Of course, he was a deputy. It was his duty to keep the citizens of the county safe, and sometimes that included things like this. Right? Levi might not agree. Oh, to hell with Levi and all the rest of them. The real truth was that he wanted to go, and so he would. That had to be good enough.

10

"I REALLY DO APPRECIATE THIS," SHILOH SAID, realizing that she'd already said it several times. Her heart swelled in her chest as they rose higher into the mountains. It hadn't been all that long since she'd been up there, but she felt the excitement of coming back home again. It meant so much more now that she knew what it was like to be 'free,' and that even though it was wonderful in so many ways, it had its detriments.

"It's not a problem," Cash replied. He sat casually in the passenger seat, looking out the window and enjoying the view. "You sure seem comfortable on these roads."

Shiloh took the switchback turns with ease. "I grew up here, and I learned to drive in just these sorts of situations. I had to be comfortable with the narrow roads and the sheer drop-offs early on, or else I don't think I ever would've gotten behind the wheel."

"Probably didn't hurt that you knew you had wings to back you up," Cash joked.

She smiled at that, feeling comfortable with him. "Yeah, probably not."

"Can I ask you something?"

"I'm sure you will anyway, and I suppose I'm a bit of a captive audience," she replied. When Shiloh had asked Cash to come up there with her, she'd wondered if it was a mistake. After all, he'd been hard to resist. She'd already told him that she hadn't wanted a relationship with him, and it hadn't been all that easy to let him go. Now, being stuck in a car with him for a long drive, she wondered just how much self-control she had. If it hadn't been for the nature of the roads, she might very well have driven right off the cliff if she let herself study his square jaw, the aquiline nose, the deep softness of his eyes.

He'd misunderstood her when she'd asked him to join her on this trip. She couldn't blame him for that, and the spark of interest in his eyes had reignited the very thing inside her that she'd been trying to snuff out. Granted, it had been a little easier to ignore the idea of finding a mate when she'd realized she had to worry not only about keeping her dragon a secret, but also about her safety.

"Why didn't you and your aunt live in town?" Cash asked. "I mean, I completely understand being in the middle of nowhere while you're young and learning how to shift. And I'm sure it's even more complicated since you're a much larger form than a wolf. While growing up, we learned in the back yard and even in the living room. But I mean, once you were older, wouldn't it have been easier for you to just live in town?"

Shiloh sighed, but it wasn't one of impatience. It was one of wistfulness, remembrance, and something else she couldn't explain. "Adelaide had been living in that cabin for most of her life when I came to stay with her. She talked to me a lot about how much safer we were if we stayed on our own, and how there just weren't many people like us left in the world. I can't tell you how many times she reminded me that she and I were the last of our family and our clan. She insisted that no one could know where the cabin was. She always liked to say that people only showed up if they were lost.

"There were a few rare occasions when a random hiker would stumble onto our property. Adelaide would give them some food and send them heading in the right direction, but she always kept them out of the house itself and sent them packing as quickly as possible. Nothing ever came of any of those encounters, but she'd always spend the next few days fretting." She smiled a little at the memory. Adelaide had been an unusual woman, but in all the best ways.

"Didn't you have to come into town for supplies and things?" Cash asked.

"Sure." Shiloh tapped her fingers on the steering wheel as she urged the car around the next turn. They were getting close now. A small piece of her wished that this wasn't a trip to retrieve the last of her items, but a trip home to introduce Aunt Adelaide to the man she'd met. No, she reminded herself. She couldn't possibly think of Cash that way, no matter how her dragon felt about him. "That was probably the only reason Adelaide let me learn to drive, I think. We grew and hunted a lot of our own food, but there are just some things you can't get from the woods. But again, a trip to town would have her fussing and worrying for days, wondering if someone had sniffed us out while we were there."

"I can't imagine that anyone would care that much about you being a dragon. I mean, other shifters, anyway," he added. "Humans wouldn't know unless you showed them. None of them have ever suspected me of having a lupine side."

Shiloh lifted a shoulder and let it fall. Why was Cash so easy to talk to? She'd spent her whole life with this big secret, yet she felt as though she could just sit there and tell him everything. "She was convinced otherwise, but she didn't like to talk about it."

Cash nodded. "I've known some older folks like that. I don't think they understand that it's not kept under wraps the same way it used to be. Sure, we don't announce it to the world, but areas like Sheridan just have a different attitude about it."

"Here we are." Shiloh flicked her turn signal.

"Are you sure? That looks like a solid tree line." Cash leaned forward in his seat, trying to look.

Shiloh smiled. "Like I said, no one was supposed to know about it." She swung confidently into the turn. The branches that overhung the old roadway swept the sides of the car, but they didn't stop it from moving forward. The chunks of rock that were sunken into the driveway and kept it from washing out had been there forever, and Shiloh slowed down to accommodate for the bumps and dips. Too narrow to let another car pass going the other direction, it was the type of road that passersby wouldn't attempt even if they happened to see it, sure that they'd get stuck. Shiloh knew that most of that was an illusion.

She slowly made her way around the final curve, and the property itself opened up in front of them. It was a small but sturdy cabin with a covered front porch. Pine trees rose protectively on either side of the structure, and a small shed out back housed their gardening equipment. The windows had been shuttered against the elements, but Shiloh knew what a scenic view they had of the surrounding mountainside. If they'd been open and the few weeds that had grown in the flower bed were plucked, it would be hard to tell that Shiloh and Adelaide no longer lived there.

"I know it's not much," she said as she got out and walked up the steps, flipping to the appropriate key on her ring. "I did love it in a lot of ways, though, and—"

"What's wrong?" Cash had lingered slightly behind her, looking around, but he moved closer at seeing the way she stiffened up.

"Someone's been here," Shiloh whispered. Her blood thundered in her ears, and her dragon was in a frenzy. "The latch is broken."

"I'll go in first," Cash suggested. "You stay here."

"No." Shiloh understood that his reaction was due to the line of work he was in, but she needed to see for herself. She couldn't just stand out there and wait. I'm going in, too."

His chest swelled a little, and Shiloh sensed some undomesticated urge to protect moving through him. She was fully prepared to argue, or even to shove him aside and tell him she would handle this herself, but Cash nodded. "Fine. We'll go in together."

Her hands shook as she stepped through the doorway. The hardwood floors were littered with papers, books, and broken ceramics. The shelves and cabinets had been completely cleared, and drawers had been overturned. Even the couch had been pulled out, and the carefully preserved jars of strawberry jelly had been smashed on the floor. "I can't believe it," she whispered, tears coming to her eyes. "It's been completely ransacked."

Cash moved carefully through the debris as he checked the two bedrooms and the bathroom. "Whoever did it is gone, at least."

"That's no great comfort," she snapped as she bent to retrieve a broken picture frame from the floor. “If they were here, then at least I could bite their heads off. Literally.”

He nodded, but he didn’t say anything more about that. “Is there anything here of value? Anything that someone would be looking for?”

Shiloh put the framed photo of herself and Aunt Adeline back on the mantel where it belonged. It felt like a ridiculously small act when it would take so much to right everything, but she couldn’t just let it fall back to the floor. She flipped her hands helplessly in the air. “I don’t think so. Everything here is old, but there aren’t any priceless antiques. I just don’t understand why anyone would do such a thing. I feel sick.” She plopped down on the couch and bent forward slightly as her stomach heaved.

“There isn’t always a good explanation,” Cash said with a sigh. “Sometimes people just take advantage of a situation and try to get whatever they can out of it. They were probably hoping to find some hidden jewelry or money.”

Shiloh swept her hands up and down her face, trying to figure out how she could accept this. “I just don’t understand. How could this have happened? I guess Adelaide was right.”

“What do you mean?” Cash found the broom

next to the fridge and began sweeping up the smashed plates on the kitchen floor.

She wanted to tell him to stop, but she knew he was only trying to help. "I thought she was being too protective with the way she talked about our house. She was concerned about people finding it, but I didn't think there was any way they ever could. I guess that's the same attitude each of us always had about our shifter sides, too. Maybe I shouldn't have moved away." Shiloh had always believed everything would be fine and that Adelaide was too worried. Her aunt thought otherwise.

"Whatever happened here, you can't take it personally," Cash advised. "I haven't been with law enforcement all that long, but one thing I have learned is that sometimes bad things just happen. You can't always find the rhyme and reason behind it. We can file a report, but most of the time, we never catch the intruders."

Shiloh shook her head as she stood. "Maybe not, but I just hate this. Adelaide would be so upset." She moved forward to start picking up the wreckage, but the corner of the area rug had been curled up when someone had pulled the couch away from the wall. It caught Shiloh's toe and sent her pitching forward. Her hands flew out and she caught herself on the coffee table as Cash dropped the broom and came rushing over.

"Are you all right?"

"God *damn* it!" she growled as she straightened up, angry at everything right now. She wanted to lash out at the bastards who did this, but of course, that was impossible. "Fucking rug! Fucking assholes!"

Cash took her hands and held them until she looked up into his eyes. His gaze was soft and concerned. "For what it's worth, I'm really sorry. We can get this cleaned up as best we can for now."

She gripped his fingers and fought the urge to throw herself against him and sob into his chest. Instead, she nodded and turned away, wiping a tear from her eye. "Yeah. You're right. No sense in moping around. I'll just—hang on."

Shiloh had bent down to flick the rug back into place so she wouldn't trip over it again. The last thing she needed was yet another reason for Cash to come to her rescue, even though she'd practically asked him to do just that when she'd invited him up there in the first place. But she noticed that the floor under the rug had been cut into a small door. The boards had been carved away to allow for a metal ring that folded flat down into the flooring and served as a latch. "Here. Help me move this coffee table."

Together, they shoved the solid wood coffee table aside so that Shiloh could push the rug completely out of the way. Lifting the door, Shiloh found a small compartment under the floor. Inside was a carved wooden box.

Cash knelt next to her and studied her face. "Did you know that was there?"

"No," she breathed as she retrieved the box and set it in her lap. It was mostly covered in dust, but some of it had been cleared away as though someone had touched it not all that long ago. Disregarding the dirt and dust that it spread on her hands and jeans, Shiloh carefully opened the box.

Inside was a familiar key. Shiloh smiled as she lifted its chain and placed it over her head. "Aunt Adelaide wore this all the time. She must've put it away sometime before she died. I hadn't noticed." She felt the presence of her beloved aunt wrap around her as she touched the cold metal.

"There's something else," Cash said softly.

The piece of paper was old and yellowed, and it nearly blended in with the inside of the box. Shiloh carefully flattened it, and another piece of paper slipped out of its folds. "It's a map and a note." She blinked tears from her eyes as she instantly recognized Adelaide's scrawled handwriting.

My dear Shiloh,

You've been such a blessing to me. I ache for your parents' loss, as that was so unnecessary, but it gave me the chance to raise a sweet little girl of my own. I love you more than I could ever explain.

Please always remember that most of the world isn't a safe place, and not everyone is kind. I know I've told you that a thousand times, but it really is true. There are those who would seek to harm you if they understood who you truly were, and I made it my life's goal to protect you from them. I hope I've done a good enough job that you'll be safe even after my death.

You are the last of us, my dear. You alone hold the key to any future that our clan might have, and we all trust you with it.

I love you.

Adelaide

. . .

Shiloh slowly put the map and the note back in the box and sat quietly on the floor. Only a moment ago, she'd been ready to clean up all the wreckage around her, but now she felt so drained, she didn't even know if she could stand up. "I think I'm ready to go home."

11

CASH SAW HIS KNUCKLES WHITEN ON THE STEERING wheel and loosened his grip. He'd volunteered to drive back down from the mountains after seeing what a state Shiloh was in. He didn't mind the narrow mountain roads, but the scene at the cabin wasn't sitting well with his wolf. It hurt Shiloh to see her childhood home pillaged, and she'd broken down even further when she'd found that little box under the floor. Tears still slid silently down her cheeks as they coasted towards Sheridan.

"You okay?" he said into the silence. "I mean, considering."

"I guess so." Shiloh looked out the window and away from him.

Damn it. There was so much he wanted to do for

her. This urge to keep her safe—an urge he couldn't convince himself had anything to do with his position as a deputy—had reared its head inside him as soon as they'd discovered someone had broken into the cabin. He'd been angry on her behalf when he'd seen the wreckage that awaited them, and then he'd rushed to her side when she'd tripped on the rug. He kicked himself for feeling this way about her. She didn't want him, and she'd made that clear, but his instincts were telling him otherwise. Now he sat there in the driver's seat, trying to find some way to make conversation.

"Is there anything I can do?" he asked quietly.

Shiloh pulled in a deep breath and wiped her face. Her eyes were swollen from crying. She'd looked tired and withdrawn when he'd seen her at the diner, but seeing her in this state was even worse. She was trying to rally herself, though, and she swallowed as she opened the box and ran her fingers over the papers inside without unfolding them. "No, but thank you. I just need to remind myself that these things happen. People see their older relatives die, and then they have to find a way to move on. It's not always easy, and it doesn't always make sense, but that's life. Right?"

"Right." He could certainly testify to life not

making any sense. If it did, then he never would've had that terrible accident that left him with a broken arm and permanent damage that kept him from roping. He wouldn't be working for the sheriff's department. But then, would that mean he never would've met Shiloh? Cash couldn't say for sure, and he didn't think he wanted to know. "What do you think that map is all about?"

"I don't know." Shiloh removed it from the box once again. She turned it one way and then the other as she studied it. This wasn't the typical map sold in town for tourists to find all the best hiking routes. It was drawn by hand, and most of it didn't appear to be labeled. "The cabin is on here," she said, pointing to the corner of the map, "but I don't think it's to scale. This part right here looks like Cloud Peak."

Cash pursed his lips. "Did you and your aunt go hiking or camping a lot?"

He already knew the answer before she shook her head. "Not really. We'd fly out in that direction sometimes. This is definitely that area because I recognize the lakes." She held up the map and pointed to several blue blobs that indicated the mountaintop water features.

"Whatever it's about, it must be special, or it

wouldn't have been hidden the way it was," Cash noted. He couldn't help it, but he was intrigued by the map. He wanted to understand it. Even though he wasn't the best deputy in the county, he still did have a deep-seated compulsion to unravel any problems that he could.

Shiloh nodded. She wasn't crying anymore, probably because she was distracted by the mystery of the map. "What's interesting, though, is I don't think Adelaide made this map. This isn't her handwriting. Whoever drew it must have had some reason for needing to get back to Cloud Peak."

He could practically taste the intrigue on his tongue. His grip was getting tight on the steering wheel once again. "Are you going to go?"

Shiloh brushed a strand of hair behind her ear. She tipped her head as she looked at the map, and then she looked up through the windshield. Squinting into the bright sunlight for a long moment, she finally nodded. "Yeah."

"I'll go with you," he volunteered instantly.

"You will?" Shiloh turned to him, her brows meeting in the middle.

He couldn't blame her for being stunned. Whatever their relationship was, it didn't require him to go take a long, difficult hike through the mountains on some wild goose chase for who-knew-what. "Sure," he said with a shrug. "I mean, that way, you don't have to go by yourself. And I'm always up for an adventure."

"Right." Shiloh stared at the map again. He thought she might tell him she could damn well go by herself if she wanted to, and he couldn't argue with that, but she just nodded as if confirming something to herself. "Right."

"I've got work for the next few days, but we could go sometime soon," he pressed. "Just let me know when you're available."

Shiloh looked too distracted to think about the details and logistics, but she absently bobbed her head once again.

Apprehension built inside Cash as he rode the brakes down the mountain. He knew some of the area around Cloud Peak, and it was a long trail in any way you went. That meant not only another long drive together up into the mountains, but also a lot of time walking side-by-side or one after the other on a trail. It could, depending on exactly where they were going, also mean camping underneath the stars.

Cash cursed himself for volunteering. He could try to justify it all he wanted, saying to himself that he was just doing this to be a good friend. He could even take the more old-fashioned approach and say that a woman really shouldn't be hiking alone in the mountains, dragon or no. There was even the idea that it was his responsibility to make sure she was safe simply because he was a deputy, even if he wasn't on duty at the moment.

The truth, though, swirled through him. His body called out for her as she sat next to him mere inches away, studying the map. Cash's very soul craved to be near her, and it was too easy to imagine what it might be like to climb into a tent with her at night. He knew he could find plenty to keep himself distracted from the hardness of the ground beneath them. His jaw tightened as he saw her naked before him in his mind's eye, her golden waves of hair falling across her shoulders and her breasts, and his pants were suddenly a little too tight.

"Interesting," Shiloh said, breaking into his thoughts as she traced her finger on the map. She had her phone on in her lap, and she was comparing the satellite images of the hiking trails to what had been scrawled out on the piece of paper. "Some of this trail is the same thing you see on any of the typical hiking maps, but not all of it. It's like there's this extra spur going off the side. I wonder if that's intentional or just a mistake from an inexperienced mapmaker. Either way, it looks like we'll get to explore some of the lake area. It's just beautiful from the air, and I wouldn't mind getting to explore it on two legs and get a different angle."

She was starting to get excited again, and that didn't make things any easier on Cash. He fed off that enthusiasm inside her. He could swear it stirred up her dragon, and that only made his wolf try all the harder to reach out for her. Damn it. He'd already agreed to the trip, and he was just going to make more trouble for himself.

12

SHILOH SAT ON THE EDGE OF HER COUCH AND STARED at the clock. She had to get down to Cowpunch Coffee in the next few minutes to start her shift. The early breakfast shift was over, but there were still plenty of folks who came in during the midmorning hours for bacon and eggs before the nine-to-five workers started flooding in for hamburgers and soup. She was going to be late.

That didn't sit well with her, but nothing seemed to be. Her stomach was flipping like an Olympic gymnast inside her, and her muscles felt as though they'd become detached from her bones. She just didn't have the energy to get up and get going, yet there were so many things she needed to do. Every time she stood, her head started spinning and she had to sit again.

Not wanting to lose her job, she hoisted herself up off the couch. Steadying herself for a minute to make sure she wouldn't collapse, she grabbed her purse. Shiloh tried not to think too much about how good it would feel to go back to bed and pull the covers over her head.

Alexis was out in the hall, pouring a cup of water into a sad potted plant that stood near the one window in this part of the building. "Hey, girl!" she said, far too loudly for the early hour. "I haven't seen you much lately. You been okay?"

"Well enough." Shiloh didn't feel like going over the details of her cabin trip with Cash. Alexis would eat it up, especially the part about how sweet Cash was. But that was exactly why Shiloh didn't want to rehash it all right now. Cash was wonderful. He'd been concerned for her safety when they'd realized the cabin had been ravaged, and he'd come rushing to her when she'd fallen. Even the tiniest things, like sweeping the kitchen floor, seemed just as important as him offering to hike up to Cloud Peak with her. "I've just been busy."

"Well, tell me you're not busy on Saturday night! Dan and I are getting together with a big group of friends. We're talking dinner, dancing, drinking. Wherever the night takes us. And I have to admit, there are some pretty cute single guys in our group, so you just might meet someone to distract you from Deputy Dog."

Shiloh made a face about that last remark, but she let it go. Alexis had no idea that Shiloh's body and soul still longed for Cash in a way that was hard to resist. He hadn't made it any easier by being so supportive and helpful when he'd gone to the cabin with her. When she'd asked him, she'd truly thought she meant it simply as a favor for a friend. Shiloh wasn't sure that Cash was thinking about it that way, and she wasn't entirely sure that she was, either.

But thinking of Cash reminded her of exactly why she couldn't go on Saturday. "I have something planned during the day, but I don't know how long it'll take."

Alexis tipped her head to the side and blinked. "That sounds mysterious. Are you going to fill me in, or is it a secret date with a stranger?" She gave Shiloh a knowing smile.

"No, just...um, a hiking trip with a friend up in the mountains." Shiloh really liked Alexis, and it was tempting to spill her guts completely. Of course, that would probably take far more time than either of them had. And it would mean Shiloh would want to know the details of what, exactly, was happening between Shiloh and Cash, and how was she going to explain that when she didn't know herself?

"If you get done early and you're not too tired, give me a call and we'll meet up. It's not a big deal even if you decide to join us late. I'd love to introduce you to more of the nightlife Sheridan has to offer," Alexis said with a wink.

"I will. I'd better be getting to work right now, though, or Barb will kill me."

Alexis put her hand on Shiloh's arm as she passed her in the hallway. She looked at her closely, concern washing over her face. "You sure you're all right?"

"Yeah. I just didn't sleep well. I'll give you a call later."

Shiloh headed to Cowpunch Coffee, wondering how she was going to get through the day. Just standing in the hall and talking with Alexis for a few minutes had nearly wiped her out. The scent of coffee and fried bacon when she walked through the door didn't do anything to rally her, though. She put her hand over her mouth and headed straight into the bathroom.

A knock came on the door a few minutes later. "Shiloh, honey. It's Barb. Are you all right?"

Shiloh splashed cold water on her face, concentrating on how nice it felt against the heat that raged inside her body. She wasn't shivering, and she didn't think she had a fever, but she was so hot, she thought she might suffocate. Her stomach had settled considerably, though. "I think I'm okay," she said weakly as she opened the door. "I'm just not feeling well this morning, but it's already a little better."

Barb peered into her face with the same scrutiny Alexis had. "Why don't you come sit in my office for a minute?"

"Oh, that's okay—"

"I'm not having a sick waitress working the dining room," Barb said with the authority of a grandmother. Her orthopedic shoes shuffled against the linoleum as she held open the office door, revealing the small room that held little more than a desk, a few chairs, and some filing cabinets. "Just have a seat and at least give yourself a few minutes before you try to get back home."

"But I'm supposed to work," Shiloh argued.

Barb was already shaking her head before she could get the entire sentence out. "I don't think so, honey. I know you're young and hungry, and you want to make as much money as you can just like everyone else, but there comes a point when it's not worth it. Your health is worth a lot more." She hesitated for a moment as her eyes swept over Shiloh.

"What?" Shiloh raised a self-conscious hand to her face, wondering just how bad she looked.

Barb pursed her lips in thought and then nodded. "I have something in mind that might help you. Stay here, and I'll run next door to the pharmacy and get it." She turned and shut the door before Shiloh had a chance to argue.

Shiloh sank into a chair and tipped her head back, grateful for the chance to get off her feet. It was odd to have someone who was practically a stranger insist on taking care of her, but then again, that was how much of her time in Sheridan had been going so far. Alexis had been a great neighbor, who'd taken her out on the town and even helped paint the kitchen. Her boyfriend Dan had been quick to stand up for her and chase those horrible men away. Cash was a story in and of himself, regardless of the tryst that had been their first date. Now there was Barb, who was treating Shiloh not merely like an employee, but one of her own. Tears spilled from the corners of Shiloh's eyes just thinking about it, and she wasn't sure she could stop them.

Her boss returned shortly, holding a small plastic bag from the pharmacy. She handed it over to her employee without a word.

Shiloh looked inside. Her stomach had been feeling better, but it dropped straight to the floor when she saw what was in the bag. "A pregnancy test?"

Barb nodded. "I figured you might not feel comfortable buying one yourself, so this was the easiest way. I don't mind seeing the funny look on the cashier's face when she sees an old woman buying one." She chuckled a bit to herself.

"I don't think…" Shiloh stopped. She really hadn't even dreamed about being pregnant, but it wasn't beyond the realm of possibility. In her mind, she started going through all the symptoms she'd been experiencing. Could it be?

"It's worth finding out." Barb perched herself on the corner of the desk and looked kindly down at Shiloh. "Even if you went to the doctor, this is the first thing they'd want to know. Just go take it, and then take the rest of the day off."

Her throat so tight she could hardly breathe, Shiloh headed back into the employee bathroom.

Her eyes blurred as she tried to read the instructions, and her hands shook as she opened the packaging. She hadn't been completely isolated from the world when she'd lived with Adelaide, but this was certainly nothing she'd experienced before. Shiloh pored over the thick folded paper that came in the box, reading it all in awe and horror that such a simple process could decide the rest of her life.

She set a timer on her phone. It wasn't all that long. If she'd been doing anything else, it would've flown by. Now, purposely not looking at the little stick, it was an eternity.

In her mind, she went over all the possibilities. Of course, she wasn't ready for something like this. There would be immense relief if it turned out Barb was wrong. But what if she were right? What would Shiloh do? She'd seen enough television to know that women in this situation often worried about what the father would say, what he would do, or if she would be all alone as she tried to raise a child. Shiloh couldn't imagine Cash doing anything other than what he'd already done when they'd gone to the cabin. He'd catch her before she fell, he'd hold her and offer all his help. He'd be right there with her, day after day, at her side.

She should be grateful, but there was still so

much more that Shiloh wanted to do on her own. That meant without a mate, and without a child. This couldn't happen. Not right now.

The timer went off, making her jump. Shiloh swallowed. She took a deep breath and then looked at the little window on the plastic stick. She checked the lines against the ones on the instructions, and then she checked again.

Sweeping everything into the trash can, Shiloh washed her hands and stared at herself in the mirror. She didn't look any different, other than the dark shadows under her eyes and the way the corners of her mouth seemed permanently dragged down.

Barb was waiting for her when she stepped out of the bathroom. Her kind eyes were inquisitive, and she saw the answer written all over Shiloh's face. She folded Shiloh into her arms and held her for a long moment there in the back corner of the kitchen. "Can I give you a bit of advice?" she asked quietly.

Shiloh nodded as she leaned into the embrace. Barb had been simply her boss until that day, but now she felt such comfort in the warm softness of the older woman.

"I don't know all your circumstances, honey, but I can say that women have been doing this for ages.

You can do this, and I'm right here for you. Anything you need, you just ask. What you need to do for today, though, is go home and rest. Give yourself some time. Okay?"

Shiloh nodded again. She wanted to thank Barb, not simply for being observant and insistent enough to go buy the pregnancy test, but for being so kind and generous when she had no obligation to be. She wanted to thank her for somehow knowing that Shiloh didn't have a mother figure in her life anymore, and the help that Barb had given her meant so much. She couldn't seem to make a single syllable come out of her mouth, though, and so she grabbed her purse and headed for home.

Those two tiny lines on the pregnancy test had given her a lot to think about. Tears leaked down her face as she got back in her car and made the drive back to her apartment. She just wanted to figure out who she was and live a life for herself, yet now she was going to bring a new life into the world.

Back home, lying on her couch and staring at the ceiling, she picked up her cell phone. Shiloh pulled up Cash's number, but she backed out to the home screen and set the phone down. She had time to figure this all out, and she wasn't ready to deal with any of it just yet.

13

Cash scratched his head as he looked around his place and tried to figure out if he was missing anything. He'd grown up near the mountains, and he'd taken more than one trip up the winding roads in a vehicle and on the gorgeous hiking trails on foot. He'd also spent a decent amount of time running through that wilderness as a wolf, when he had the time and the privacy. That all meant he was pretty qualified for a day out on the trail. His experience in seeing how many lost hikers and tourists had to be rescued made him second-guess himself despite the fact that he could shift and hunt down some game if he got hungry enough.

The idea of being out there with Shiloh had been haunting him all week, and now that it was finally coming, he felt a shiver of anticipation run down his spine. She hadn't called to cancel or to tell him that she wanted to go alone. He'd even texted her that morning to make sure she was still good to go, just to make sure. This was happening.

He gave a thought for Wade as he headed out to his truck. His friend had advised him to be a part of Shiloh's life, even if it was as friends. That guidance had seemed completely ridiculous at the time, because Cash had known that he wanted to be so much more with Shiloh. It had happened of its own accord, though, and Cash was starting to see the wisdom in it. The more time they spent together—even without any expectation of being romantic—the more chance he had of Shiloh changing her mind about him.

With all of this in his thoughts, he was bright and eager as he picked her up at her apartment. Shiloh, however, looked completely miserable as she dragged herself up into the passenger seat of his truck. There were dark circles under her eyes, and her shoulders were sagging.

"Are you all right?" Cash put the truck in reverse, but he didn't let go of the brake just yet. "Want me to stop somewhere for coffee?"

She made a face and shook her head. "Oh God, no. I don't think I could stand any coffee right now."

Backing out onto the street, Cash was starting to have some doubts about this trip. "Just too early for you, then? I figured you were used to getting up early with your job."

His gentle ribbing went over like a lead balloon. Shiloh merely pulled a package of crackers out of her bag and began slowly munching on them. "I'm fine."

They were gliding through downtown now, with hardly any traffic out on the streets yet. Cash still had his concerns. "If you're not feeling good, we can just do this another time."

"No," she snapped. "I've got to do this now. We've already got it all settled out and have the days off work, and who knows when that will happen again. I'm just a little under the weather this morning, but I'll be fine in a bit."

Cash's wolf was on full alert. He didn't like this. She clearly didn't feel well, and he had the distinct feeling that she was keeping something from him. He could write off her crabbiness as just a result of not feeling well, but he certainly missed the bold, brassy personality that seemed to have slowly drifted away from her.

He remained quiet as they drove past the city limits, but his worries still gnawed at him as the road's incline became a little steeper. Cash glanced over at her, seeing that although she was no longer munching the crackers, she still hadn't perked up. "I don't want to push you, Shiloh, but I'm worried. This is a long trail we're going to be doing today. If you start feeling worse in the middle of it, then it could put us in quite a predicament."

She waved a dismissive hand without looking at him. "I could just shift and fly out of there if I wanted to."

"And if you wanted to, you could also just shift and fly your ass up the mountain, too," he pointed out, irritation replacing his concern. Cash was starting to wonder why he'd agreed to this in the first place. Had he been so desperate just to spend time with her that he was going to not only sacrifice an entire day off, but also spend it hoofing up a trail in the mountains? Looking at it now, he could see just how desperate it looked. "It's fine if you don't feel good, but you don't have to be a hero."

"I'm not!" She folded her arms over her stomach, but she pulled them right back off and shifted uncomfortably in her seat.

"Then are you mad at me for something?" Cash

pressed. "You're treating me like I did something wrong here, but I sure as hell don't know what it is. I'd rather you just tell me. Hell, I'd rather you chew me the fuck out and tear me a new one than just leave me hanging while you grumble at me." He tightened his grip on the wheel, but the roads were still the long, smooth ones of the foothills.

Shiloh closed her eyes and sucked in a deep breath. She took a sip from her water bottle. It seemed as though she wasn't going to speak at all, but he sensed her gathering up her thoughts and taming her inner dragon. "I'm not angry with you," she finally said, her voice barely above a whisper. Cash had to strain to hear it above the sound of the engine. "You've been nothing but kind, and I'm sorry I snapped at you. I've just had a lot on my mind. My stomach was a little upset this morning, but it's getting better. I promise."

His wolf backed down a bit, and he felt some of his anger subsiding. Cash hadn't ever thought he would fall for someone so hard, and he was making a fool of himself. That was his fault, not hers. He didn't understand why she didn't seem to feel the same bond between their shifter selves that he did, but there was always a chance that he'd been wrong. "If you're sure," he mumbled.

"I am." Shiloh sat up a little straighter in her seat. She adjusted the seatbelt as though it were too restricting, but she didn't complain about it. "If you really are curious, I did think about just shifting and flying up to Cloud Peak. It would be faster, and I wouldn't have to bother you."

"It's not a bother," he insisted instantly. So much for not wanting to sound desperate.

She shot him a grateful look. "I spent a lot of time looking at that map. There are some small landmarks on it that I'm not sure I'd see from the air. It looks like it was intended to be followed on foot. Just because I *can* do it in my other form doesn't mean that's the best way. I don't know what any of it means or what we're going to find, but I don't want to risk missing something just because I tried to do it the easy way."

"That's understandable." Cash glanced at her again. He didn't mind looking at her at all, not with the beauty of her golden hair and the light in her eyes. Now though, he just wanted to make sure she was all right. The last thing he wanted was for her to put on a brave face. As he took a peek at her, he noticed the chain around her neck. "Is that the key you found in the box?"

She lifted it out from where it had been tucked

inside her shirt and studied it. The thing was old and solid, the metal tarnished, but the top was decorated with fine filigree work. "Yeah. Aunt Adelaide wore it all the time. I don't think I'd ever seen her without it. She must've taken it off at some point before she died, but I hadn't noticed. I felt kind of bad when I realized that, but I'm also glad she kept it aside for me. It's a special thing to remember her by, and I can have it with me all the time."

Cash couldn't help but smile at the sentiment. Shiloh had grown up without the benefits of a real clan, but that didn't mean she'd missed out on having a close relationship. "That's nice."

They drove along in silence for a while as they headed up further into the mountains. Cash could sense that she was still a little tired, but she didn't seem to be nearly as bad off as she'd been when he'd first picked her up. That gave him hope for the rest of the trip. Shiloh had mentioned earlier that she'd had a lot on her mind, and he considered asking her about it. He just wanted to help if there was any way he could, but he decided it was probably safer if he just let it go for now. They'd made their peace with each other, so why push it?

Finally, they reached the parking lot at the trailhead. This was as far as they could go by vehicle, and they'd be on foot from there. He had no qualms about the long walk and a chance at getting Shiloh to open up a little more, but something else didn't sit right with him. There were only a few vehicles in the parking lot that early in the day, but there was a group of them at the back of the parking lot that he recognized instantly. Cash hesitated only for a moment in the entryway before he swung into a parking space.

"You okay?" Shiloh had noticed the difference in him, even though he'd tried not to let her know anything was wrong.

"I'm fine." Cash got out and retrieved his backpack from the back seat. He looked at the small collection of vehicles through the rear windshield, hoping that somehow he'd been wrong the first time. Nope. There was no mistaking the two small campers and the beat-up trucks that hauled them. Cash was on an even keel with Shiloh now, and he didn't want to do anything to mess that up. "I just thought I recognized some of the vehicles here, but I was mistaken."

"Oh." She pulled her pack on and adjusted the straps on her shoulders. "I guess you probably know just about everyone around here, don't you?"

"There are always plenty of tourists, and lots of

people come up into the Big Horns to explore," he replied as he locked the truck. They moved across the parking lot toward the trailhead, and he studied the campers once again. There was no sign that anyone was in them, but he couldn't be certain unless he went knocking on the camper doors. He watched carefully as they passed by, but he didn't see any sign of the slim man with the crossbow tattoo. Once again, the only thing he had to go on was a gut feeling, and that wasn't going to get him far.

Deciding it was a better idea to leave work behind and concentrate only on his time with Shiloh, he hitched his backpack up a little higher on his shoulders. "You've got the map?"

"Right here," she affirmed as she pulled it out of a pocket of her backpack. "Let's get started."

14

THE DAY WAS WARM, BUT A CONSISTENT BREEZE KEPT the moisture wicked from the back of Shiloh's neck. As they moved along the trail, she started to realize that maybe getting out of the house and back out into nature was exactly what she needed to make herself feel better. Her worries about the future faded into the background as she focused on the way her hiking boots hit the grass and rocks under her feet. Her muscles thrived from the chance to get out and move, not just threading between tables while carrying trays, but really getting a workout. She found herself smiling, which she definitely hadn't expected when she'd started her day bent over the toilet.

"This is gorgeous," she said as they came around

a slight bend. "I've always loved the view from the air, but there's a completely different perspective from here. I love it."

"Mmmhmm."

"We're making good headway, but it's hard to tell from the map just how far we'll have to go. I went to the library and pulled up some satellite images of the area to see what I could figure out. Well, the librarian had to help me, but she was great. Anyway, I think once we get past the lakes, we'll have to decide whether we stay on the main trail or if there's a separate one we're supposed to take." She marched forward, unhindered by the weight on her back or the length of their journey.

"Mmmhmm."

She was walking slightly ahead of him, and now she frowned. Once she'd gotten past her bad mood —which had just been the result of her queasy stomach forcing her to think about the fact that she was pregnant—she'd been more than ready to head out on this adventure. Shiloh had even been surprised to find that she was happy to do it with Cash at her side. The smoldering intensity of whatever they had between them was a bit intimidating, but she couldn't deny the fact that he was a nice guy. He was the perfect candidate for the trip, and seeing what the map had to show them would be a marvelous tribute to Aunt Adelaide.

But something had changed in him. "Are you all right?"

"Mmmhmm."

"Are you sure? You got kind of quiet and weird as soon as we parked, and it's only gotten worse," Shiloh pointed out. "You've hardly said a word. In fact, I don't think you've said *a* word at all, because I'm pretty sure 'mmmhmm' isn't in the dictionary." She turned around and walked backward on the trail so she could see him.

He fought back a smile and looked off to the side, obviously trying not to let her see that she'd gotten to him with her humor. "We'll have to look it up when we get back, and then we'll see."

She smiled at him now, and her dragon soared a little at seeing the softness in his eyes when he looked at her. Shiloh tried to repress it, but it could always just be a friendly look. Right? "Something's bothering you. I'd let it go, but you weren't nice enough to let me keep my bad mood."

Cash raised one eyebrow. "I'll be sure not to make the same mistake next time."

"Come on! We've got hours ahead of us. If I have to walk the whole way and listen to you harumphing, then I might just sprout my wings and fly after all," Shiloh threatened.

His footsteps picked up their pace a little, and he was suddenly a little closer to her. The change was subtle. He wasn't even close enough for her to feel the heat of his body, yet she felt as though he'd taken her by the hips and pressed his forehead against hers as his hickory brown eyes lasered into hers. "Maybe I'd like to see that," he said.

She could taste adrenaline on her tongue, and sparkles of electricity exploded over her skin. Shiloh turned back around so that she wouldn't have to look at him anymore, hoping that would make enough of a difference. She'd already decided that she didn't want him in her life, not like that. "You'll have to catch the freakshow some other time."

"Whoa. Hey, I didn't mean it that way." He'd closed the last bit of distance between them now, and he was right next to her on the trail.

Shit. All she'd done was lure him further toward her. "No, I know. I was just kidding. So are you going to tell me what's bothering you, or what?" Better to turn the subject back toward him.

Cash stuffed his hands in his pockets and looked ahead down the trail. "I told you I recognized some vehicles in the parking lot. I did, but they don't belong to anyone I know personally."

"Oh?"

He shrugged a little. "I was sent out on a call about some campers who were set up in a prohibited spot, and I know for sure those were the same guys."

"But they weren't doing anything illegal just then, right?" Shiloh looked around. They'd only passed one other group on the trail so far, who'd greeted them with friendly waves.

"No, and the guy I talked to was relatively cooperative and said they'd move. I just had a bad feeling about them, and it caught me off-guard to see those vehicles again. I guess I wasn't in the mood to think about work today." His eyes were sharp as he gazed off into the distance.

Shiloh realized that even though they'd spent some time together lately, most of their conversation had been focused on her. "Things not going well at the office?"

There was a wave of hesitation that she could practically see cross his mind, but then he nodded. "It's been hard to find a good balance with it. I was working the rodeo circuit for so long that it just fit flawlessly into my life. I didn't have to think about when I worked or how hard I worked because I just automatically did it. I didn't even leave that work in the arena. I carried it with me all the time, and I didn't mind."

"It was more of a way of life than a job," Shiloh concluded.

"Exactly!" His eyes widened a little at her understanding. "It isn't as though I'd never worked a typical job, but they weren't actually careers. This is totally different, and it's harder than I thought. People talk about the work itself being tough, but I actually kind of like the work. I don't mind tracking down bad guys or helping tourists find their hotels. I just can't seem to decide if I'm going to completely throw myself into the job or get so distracted that I can hardly remember the shift I just worked." Cash turned slightly away again.

Shiloh sensed there was something more to the story. She didn't quite get why she could read him that way, but on the chance that she was wrong, she didn't ask. "I'm sure that's difficult," she said instead. "I know it's not the same, but it hasn't been all that easy to go from living the secluded life in the mountains to living right in the middle of town. My 'job,' if you will, was to take care of Adelaide once she and I both got old enough that she wasn't taking care of me anymore. It wasn't like I had regular hours. Some days there would be absolutely nothing to do and I'd be bored out of my mind, and other days I'd be up at all hours trying to make sure I was giving Adelaide her medicine at the right time, getting groceries, and making sure the house was clean enough to make her happy." She smiled wryly to herself. "That makes it sound awful, but it wasn't. As much as I was looking forward to living in town, it hasn't been quite as idyllic as I thought it would be."

A troubled frown rippled across his lips. "Is everything okay?"

"Sure. It's just a lot to get used to, and..." She hesitated. Shiloh hadn't told him about the baby, and this didn't seem to be a good time. It was his problem if he didn't like the news, but it would be her problem at least until they got back down into Sheridan. The drama could wait until later.

But should she tell him about that encounter with the 'maintenance men' who'd tried to get into her apartment? Everything was fine now, and they hadn't returned, but the incident had certainly colored her experience of living out on her own. She wanted to tell Cash. Given his job, he'd probably have some good advice for her. Then again, he might get all protective again or even try to tell her she shouldn't be living alone. It was easier to let it go for the moment.

"Shiloh?" Cash prompted, still waiting for more.

"Oh, it's nothing. It's just been a lot more work than I anticipated to keep up with everything. I don't regret moving into Sheridan because if I'd stayed at the cabin, I'd still be wondering what I was missing out on." And maybe she would've been home when someone had found the place and torn it apart. Shiloh suppressed a shudder. "Anyway, the point I was trying to make is that I think I can relate. You left a way of life with the rodeo, just as I left a way of life with Adelaide. Working for someone else and trying to do what seems normal isn't as easy as I thought it would be. That's all."

"I appreciate that."

"What?"

"Just your understanding," Cash said casually. "I don't think a lot of people would have much sympathy for my situation."

"Not even your pack?" she asked absently as she pulled the map out and consulted it once again. "It's got to be nice knowing that you've always got someone to back you up. I always had Adelaide, but now that she's gone, I've just had to throw myself at the mercy of the rest of the world."

"That can't be easy," Cash said gently. "You don't have distant relatives anywhere else? Some other clan that you could at least visit with?"

Shiloh shook her head. The idea made her a little sad, but being alone in the world was something she was used to. "No. I mean, I'm sure there's some very distant cousin out there, but it's no one that I'm close to or that I've even met. It's always been just us."

Cash chewed on his lip. "In some ways, it might not be such a bad thing. There can be a lot of pressure in a pack or a clan. I've seen some groups do some pretty crazy things just because they want to impress their Alpha or because they get territorial. I've always been active in my pack, but I'm not right up there at the top. I don't have to worry about becoming the next Alpha or family politics. Sometimes I think I should do more, and I'd always be there for any of my brothers and sisters who needed me, but I still get to live my own life."

She smiled at him, only slightly jealous. Shiloh had been in such an exclusive club for such a long time that it would be hard to imagine a whole clan of dragons surrounding her. "Sounds like you've got it pretty good."

"Yeah, I think so."

The two of them walked on in silence for a while, stopping only to check rock formations against the scrawling figures on the map. Shiloh consistently found herself measuring the distance between them or studying the lines of his face. She listened to his voice, not just the words, but the deep rumble and the way it emanated from his chest. It was like a subtle song that soothed her dragon, and sometimes she found herself getting so lost in the sound of it that she hadn't paid attention to a single word he'd actually said.

This was going to be an interesting adventure, indeed.

15

THE LAND WAS ABSOLUTELY STUNNING, MAKING CASH wonder why he hadn't spent more time out there. The sky was huge above them, framed by the massive rock formations that he mostly only knew at a distance. The lakes they passed were so serene they were practically magical.

It didn't hurt that he was following just behind or next to Shiloh, depending on the trail's width at the time. He loved watching her face change as she talked about various aspects of life. She was smiling with shining eyes one moment, and then she might be frowning and chewing her lip the next. Her body moved with ease and grace along the trail, her feet easily navigating as though she'd done this a hundred times. Cash didn't know why such little details were so enchanting, but he did know he could stand just behind her and stare at the curve of her neck as she studied the map for hours.

"Okay," Shiloh said with a sigh of anticipation as she held up the old piece of paper once again. "It looks like we should be reaching Mistymoon Lake before nightfall. It looked amazing in all the pictures I looked up, and there should be some good camping spots there. I wasn't thinking about this being an overnight trip, but it looks like that's where we're at for the moment. What do you think?"

Cash felt his whole body react when she mentioned spending the night. He'd known it was a possibility, considering that this was a long trail, but just to hear those words coming from her mouth made every cell he had surge toward her. Shiloh presented such a conundrum for him. She'd said she didn't want to be with him, yet he noticed her subtle glances and the softness in her smile. They were spending so much time together, and he felt his wolf only growing more and more attached. Cash knew that simply pitching camp for the night didn't mean anything was going to happen, yet he longed to wrap his arm around her at a lakeside campfire and claim her body again.

His thoughts were distracted by a group of men

heading in their direction on the trail, coming down toward them. "I think we have company."

Shiloh stepped aside to make room for the oncoming traffic, but she stiffened as they approached.

Cash felt the same reaction happening to him. There were four men, and none of them looked like typical hikers. They wore pull-on boots or tennis shoes instead of hiking boots, and their backpacks looked like school bags picked up at a discount store. This looked more like a group of people he'd chase out of a back alley somewhere in town.

He didn't recognize three of them, but one of them was all too familiar. It was the slim man with the black baseball cap and the crossbow tattoo on his arm, the same one he'd talked to about camping in the wrong spot. Cash stepped forward to put himself between the newcomers and Shiloh. She might get mad at him for it later, but so be it. There was no obvious danger from these men, but Cash didn't feel like taking chances, not with Shiloh there.

"Howdy," the slim man said as they drew closer to each other. He nodded politely, but his bright green eyes lingered a little too long on Cash's face. "Do I know you from somewhere?"

Cash was fully aware that when he was at work, people really only saw the uniform. They didn't pay any attention to his face. "Perhaps," he answered evasively as he took several more steps up the trail.

"No, I'm pretty sure I do." The other man had stopped now, his friends gathered at his back as he clogged the trail. "I've seen you recently. You were the cop who wanted us to move our campsite."

Cash wasn't afraid of these assholes. He'd encountered plenty like them in the past, both on the rodeo circuit and in his position as deputy. He wasn't stupid, though. He knew they were totally outnumbered, alone, and he didn't have his service weapon with him. Cash eyed the odd lumps in the hefty military-style canvas bag that a large bald man carried on his back. "You're right. Good to see you again. Hope you're enjoying the mountains. They're beautiful this time of year. We'll let you get on your way now." Cash grabbed Shiloh's hand and stepped off the side of the trail to head past them.

She hadn't resisted, thank god, and he could feel her pulse pounding in her wrists.

"Hold on a second," Crossbow Tattoo said from behind them. "Maybe you can help us with something."

Damn it. The only thing Cash wanted to do was to get the hell away from these guys. They made his wolf raise its hackles, standing guard. Cash turned to look over his shoulder. "What's that?"

Crossbow smiled, but it didn't reach the rest of his face. His eyes were too busy skimming over both Cash and Shiloh, analyzing, studying. "About how far is it back down to the parking lot?"

Well, these were the kinds of questions he could answer whether he liked this creep or not. If this was really all these guys wanted to know, then he could send them on their way and stop thinking about them. Cash and Shiloh had been having a good time out on the trail, and he was ready to get back to that. "About six miles from here."

Crossbow shook his head. He lifted his hat, scratched the top of his head, and then replaced it. "Well boys, you know what that means."

The four of them had been standing there with their hands at their sides one moment, looking like complete slackers, and in a fraction of a second, they were flying at Cash and Shiloh. Cash jumped forward, once again trying to put himself between these strange men and Shiloh, but the bald man thumped him hard with an elbow to the stomach.

Cash bent forward, the wind knocked out of him, but he wasn't going to give up the fight that easily. He took a step back, letting them think he was defeated because he needed a little space.

But then his wolf came surging to the surface. Cash's skin prickled all over as hundreds of hairs began pushing through. He wouldn't dare shift if he were on duty or anywhere near other people. The secret was an important one to keep, but he would do anything to protect Shiloh from whoever these people were. Cash heard as much as felt the crunch in his skull as his fangs descended, punching through his gums and ready to sink into some bastard's throat. His hands and feet twisted and sent throbs of pain through his limbs as they turned to paws.

His senses were always magnified in his shifted form, and the first thing he noticed in the split second before he lunged at the bald man was that no one had gasped in terror at seeing the man in front of them turn into a wolf. Cash hadn't sensed that these men were shifters; they seemed completely human to him. Before he had the chance to contemplate that too deeply, he heard the twang of something metallic in the air.

Something wrapped around his body from behind. Cash felt every inch of it along his fur, and he yelped in pain. It felt like it was cutting him into sections, melting straight through his flesh and bones. He fell to the ground as wave after wave of agony ripped through him. His fangs receded. He felt the torture of his body reverting to its human form far too quickly. Cash didn't understand what was happening. He had no control, and his eyes widened as Crossbow stood over him.

He was laughing, and this time the emotion did reach his eyes. That didn't make Cash feel any better about the situation.

"Well, well. Who would've thought the dragon would befriend a wolf, boys?" Crossbow said. He was holding something that looked like a long wooden handle with a strip of metal coming out of the end.

He jerked it slightly, and Cash realized that strip of metal was wrapped around his body. That was what had sent such pain and confusion coursing through him. Cash clenched his teeth in pain, not wanting to give Crossbow the satisfaction of hearing him scream.

The bald man stepped forward and yanked a plastic tie around Cash's wrists. Crossbow flicked his wrist and made the metal strip retreat into the wooden handle. "Shifters are so funny. They think some teeth and claws make them invincible, but they don't understand they're absolutely nothing compared to modern weaponry."

"What the fuck is that thing?" Cash gasped. He still lay on the ground, recovering. His wolf had retreated completely, and he could barely feel it still inside him. Nothing like this had ever happened before. He managed to turn his head and see that Shiloh was on the ground as well, with one of the other goons tying her hands. Her eyebrows were scrunched together in pain, but she was alive and still with him.

The smirk on Crossbow's face was infuriating. "Just another reason why you animals are such funny creatures. We know better than you do how your bodies work. It turns out a nice jolt of electricity kept at just the right level makes you tuck your tail between your legs and turn right back into humans. It's much easier to deal with you like this."

Cash swallowed as he tried to wrap his head around this. "What do you want from us?"

"Not you. Really, just her." Crossbow stepped to the side and stood over Shiloh now. "Tell us where it is."

"Where *what* is?" she gasped.

Cash could see the fear on her face. He couldn't blame her at all, but it disturbed him that it ran so deep. Even with her dragon chased so thoroughly down inside her, Cash could tell that she'd been scared even before the group had attacked them. There was the way she'd stiffened when she'd seen them on the trail, and the fact that she hadn't objected to Cash taking control of the situation. Who the hell were these guys?

Crossbow rolled his eyes. "Like you don't know, you little bitch. You're going to lead us to the treasure."

Confusion and panic mingled on her face. "Treasure?"

"Looks like she's playing stupid, Tracy," the bald man said as he nudged Shiloh's knee with the toe of his boot.

Crossbow—now Tracy—shot him a dirty look, presumably for using his real name. "Nice way of paying attention to the plan, *Eric.*"

The other two goons, younger men with auburn hair that looked like they could be twins, elbowed each other and laughed.

"Fine. If nobody else is going to take this seriously, then I will." In one quick motion, Tracy whipped a pistol out from the back of his waistband and pointed it straight at Cash's forehead as he looked at Shiloh. "You have two choices, dragon. You either take us to your treasure, or you don't and I kill your little boyfriend here."

Terror stilled Shiloh. "Please, I don't know what you're talking about."

This wasn't the first time Cash had a gun pointed at his forehead. He was more pissed off than anything else, and it frustrated him to know he couldn't do anything to help Shiloh right now. With his wolf having retreated, he had no weapons left to fight with. He looked at Shiloh, willing her eyes to meet his. There were tears glimmering in them when she finally pulled her gaze away from Tracy and looked at him. Cash shook his head ever so slightly. Whoever these people were and whatever they wanted, he wasn't worth it. She shouldn't give in.

Tracy tightened his grip on the pistol. "I'm not a patient man," he warned.

A sob racked her body. "Whatever you want. Please!"

"Get them on their feet." Tracy gestured to his cohorts with the muzzle of the gun. "I need them as cooperative as possible. We'll head back to the lake and make camp for the night, and then we can go on our treasure hunt tomorrow." The men let out whoops of excitement as Shiloh and Cash were dragged to their feet and shoved up the trail.

16

SHILOH SLUMPED AGAINST CASH'S SHOULDER, grateful that at least if she had to find herself in such a terrifying situation, she could still be with someone she knew. The ropes that bound her wrists were tight, digging into her skin. The electric leash that Tracy and his henchmen had whipped around her when they'd attacked had chased her dragon to the furthest recesses of her soul, leaving her feeling completely drained as she watched the men go through her backpack.

It was Tracy himself—the same man with those penetrating green eyes who'd tried to get into her apartment—who snatched the map out of the side pocket. He jerked his wrist to shake out the folds, and Shiloh could see the greed that filled his eyes as he studied it. "So, you don't know what treasure I'm talking about, huh?" he asked as he stepped closer to the captors.

Shiloh shrugged, or at least she tried to. They'd bound her wrists and then tied her to Cash, so she wasn't capable of moving much. "It's just an old hiking map. I don't think it actually means anything." How could anyone in this day and age even be *thinking* about something like hidden treasure? It just seemed like such a fairytale idea.

Tracy bent down, bracing his elbows on his knees, and dangled the map near the ground. He forced her chin up with his free hand so that she had to look into his eyes, where she saw the campfire dancing in their depths. "Here's the deal, *dragon.* I don't believe for one second that you don't know what treasure I'm talking about, especially considering that you have a map like this. You're going to lead us to it in the morning. If you don't, I'll kill your boyfriend while you watch. I'm not just going to shoot him at point-blank range, either. I have a whole arsenal of weapons that can cause a lot of pain for a shifter, and I know how to use them. It'll be slow and painful, and you'll see every second of it. If you still don't cooperate, I'll do the same to you. I won't kill you, though. I'll just make you wish you were dead."

Cash thrust forward, fighting against his bonds. "Don't you dare touch her."

"Easy, Rover," Tracy laughed, not even bothering to back away. He grinned at Shiloh. "You've got to keep this one on a tight leash, don't you?"

Slowly, Tracy stood and headed back to the other side of the campfire, where he made himself comfortable while he studied the map.

"I'm so sorry," Shiloh whispered.

"What are you sorry for?" he replied. "This isn't your fault."

She pulled in a deep breath and let it out with a shudder, feeling like a complete fool. "Maybe not completely, but I should've figured it all out before it ever came to this, and now I've dragged you into it."

They were tied next to each other, her left knee and elbow tied to his right, so he managed to nudge his shoulder out of the way enough that he could look at her. His eyes were dark as coals, yet somehow still comforting. "They're dragon hunters, aren't they?"

She nodded, eyeing Eric as he clomped just outside of the firelight to fetch another log. "That's what I think."

"It makes sense with all these weapons they have, but I've never seen anything like them before." Cash was watching them, too. One of the twins had taken a long gun out of the canvas bag and was inspecting it, turning it this way and that in the firelight.

"Me, neither." Not that she had any experience to speak from. "I've seen these guys before, though."

His muscles hardened. "You have?"

She felt like crying all over again, but she fought hard to pull herself together. "They showed up at my apartment, pretending to be maintenance men and trying to get in. Alexis and her boyfriend came by, and that's the only reason they left. It totally freaked me out, and that was why I asked you to go to the cabin with me. I should've told you, but I was afraid you'd make a big deal out of it."

A short laugh escaped Cash as little more than a breath.

"What's so funny?"

"I've run into these assholes myself. You remember me telling you about the campers parked in the wrong spot? It was these guys. I recognized their vehicles down at the parking lot when we started on the trail, but *I* didn't want to say anything because I didn't want you to worry. I didn't have any logical reason to think they were anything more than irresponsible tourists. Turns out I was wrong. Some good detective work on my part, huh?" He let out another ironic laugh.

Shiloh leaned harder against him. They might have both been better off if they'd been honest with each other. There was still one major thing she hadn't told him yet. Considering they might not make it out of the mountains alive, Shiloh thought the news about the baby would have to wait a little longer. It was a big deal, but they had even bigger fish to fry at the moment. "Don't blame yourself. I'm the one who should've known. Adelaide was constantly harping about how there are people in the world who wanted to hurt us. I thought she meant people who would put me in a science lab and run tests on me, not dragon hunters with specialized weapons. I should've known, though. These are probably the same people who ransacked my cabin, and they'd already managed to track me down in town."

"At least we know now," Cash said with a wry smile. "Can I tell you something?"

"I'm not going anywhere," she joked. This might not be a time for humor, but Cash always brought out a little more of her natural cheekiness. He made her comfortable. Just concentrating on the way it felt to have his arm and leg pressed against hers made her feel better about their dangerous predicament.

"I was really looking forward to camping in the mountains with you," he said quietly. "I know you said you want to find yourself. I get that, and I respect that. But I can't help it. I thought a romantic hike under the stars might be just the thing for us. These guys have ruined my plans a bit, but I still have to say that the scenery is just as beautiful as the company."

Shiloh felt her face flush silently as she looked out over Mistymoon Lake. It was cradled by the mountains, and she could see the summit of Cloud Peak rising over it all, reaching toward the bright smattering of stars in the velvety night. "It could be very romantic if we weren't tied together and held hostage," she admitted. How could he make her swoon so hard that she could have amorous thoughts even when one wrong move could get her killed? Adelaide had told her once, a very long time ago, that all shifters eventually found the one person they were fated to be with. Shiloh didn't know what that was supposed to feel like, and surely she couldn't feel that way about a wolf, but he was starting to make her wonder.

Cash lifted his eyes to the stars, looking thoughtful. "They say two people who are in a difficult situation together often end up with the deepest bonds."

Shiloh pressed her cheek to his shoulder, partly for comfort and partly so she wouldn't have to look at him. Had he read her thoughts about the inexplicable connection between them, or was he just being philosophical? Ironically, Cash didn't even know just how difficult of a situation they were in, considering the life growing inside her was still her secret alone. "I think I've heard something like that before."

"Shut up!" Tracy barked from across the fire. He'd gotten up on his knees as he glared at them, his face twisted and his hand on another one of the strange guns they'd brought with them. "If I hear another peep, I'll separate you."

Shiloh clamped her tongue in her teeth. She felt Cash's hand clench around hers, and she thought she understood the message he was trying to send her. They had to stick together, because that would mean a better chance of surviving. This wasn't about romantic notions or the way they seemed to connect. It was about getting away from these hunters and getting safely back into town.

She watched as Tracy got comfortable on his side of the fire. The twins were doing the same, but big, bald Eric was on watch. He leaned against a tree with a gun in his hands, making eye contact with Shiloh every few seconds to make sure she knew she was being watched.

With little choice, the two captives leaned back and sank to the ground. The night was cool, but Shiloh was warm where her body was pressed against Cash's. She looked up at the stars, wishing they could tell her what their fate would be. She had so much she still wanted to do and so much life yet to live.

Cash kept his hand tightly around hers, his fingers moving gently against her knuckles. She focused on the slight movement, finding comfort in it even though things could go wrong at any moment. Her parents were gone. Aunt Adelaide was gone. There was no trace of her clan but herself, yet she wasn't alone. That had to be enough for now.

17

CASH WOKE WITH A START, SURPRISED THAT HE'D fallen asleep in the first place. He'd known, as he lay there next to Shiloh, that it was best to at least get some sleep while he could. That didn't mean he thought he could actually do it. That electrical device had taken a lot out of him, though, far more than getting accidentally shocked on an electric horse fence. With her curled against his side, he'd at least managed to doze off.

The sun was threatening to come up at any time. He could see the slight lightening of the navy sky along the horizon. It would take a little longer there, with the mountains surrounding their little valley, but if Tracy had been serious about taking off this morning, then he'd probably have them on their feet in less than an hour.

Cash lifted his head to look around the camp. He spotted Tracy, still snoring away in his sleeping bag with his baseball cap pulled down over his face. Eric was camped a short distance away from his boss. The big man had taken the first guard shift, but they'd changed places at some point in the night. Eric slept curled in a ball like a giant child, his arms tucked in against his chest and under his chin. One twin was sprawled out not far from him, an empty whiskey bottle on the ground next to his outstretched fingers.

The other twin was against the same tree where Eric had leaned while on guard duty. The difference was that he wasn't awake. He slumped against the trunk with a gun across his lap and his head bent slightly forward.

Cash's stomach clenched with anticipation as soon as he'd finished assessing the current scenario. "Shiloh," he whispered, hardly daring to even form the words lest someone hear them.

"I'm awake." Her own lips moved with barely a sound. Her eyes opened and looked up into his.

He saw the fear there, but also the same determination that was growing inside him. They'd been rendered completely vulnerable by those whips the day before, but now they'd had some time to recover. Cash could feel that his wolf had completely regenerated and was ready to fight, and he had little doubt that Shiloh's dragon was the same way. Instead of risking more talk that might wake the others, Cash gestured with his head toward their sleeping guard.

Shiloh peeked around him until she could see what he'd seen. She nodded her understanding, but then she lifted a shoulder. He understood. *What do we do?*

Cash was still trying to figure that out. They were still outnumbered. The only weapons they had were their inner animals, but those could be easily subdued according to how things had gone the night before. Even if they managed to shift before their captors awoke, there was a good chance they wouldn't have enough of a surprise on them to make a difference. Cash clenched his jaw as he wriggled the place where their wrists were tied together. "Claws," he mouthed.

Understanding dawned bright and beautiful in Shiloh's eyes. She closed them, concentrating. Her hand moved slightly against his, and then he felt it change. Heat flooded her body and flowed down her arm, and her bones popped slightly out of place as she allowed her hand to transform from that of a human to that of a dragon. Fine golden scales erupted and slid against his skin as her nails extended and curled, forming the sharp and slender talons of her ancient, reptilian form.

With the change completed, Shiloh twisted her arm around. Cash could feel the ropes pulling at his skin and knew it was even worse for her as she maneuvered within the confines of their bindings. The ropes shivered and shimmied, digging even further into his wrist as her claws created tension against the fibers, but Cash gritted his teeth against it. All the pain in the world was worth it if it got them out of there.

The rope around his wrist gave with a final twang. To Cash, it ricocheted through the morning air like a bullet and echoed off the mountains that surrounded them. He hesitated, waiting for the hunters to come bearing down on them. The twin against the tree who was supposed to be on duty snorted in his sleep. A line of drool ran down his chin, but he didn't open his eyes.

The initial determination he'd been feeling only built now that they were that much closer to getting away. One set of ropes falling away meant there was a little bit of slack in the binding that kept the two of them held so tightly together. Not that Cash minded being stuck with her, but he knew they'd be able to make a much more efficient run for it if they weren't the only competitors in the three-legged race. He twisted so that her claws could get to another section of rope, the one that held them together.

Shiloh worked in perfect unison with him without any actual communication, waiting for him to place the rope where she could reach it before she started sawing away with the thick blade that was her claw. As soon as it fell away, Cash reached into his pocket for a knife while Shiloh sat up. Bits of grass were stuck in her hair as she glanced around at their kidnappers, and then she set to the lengths of rope that kept their thighs pressed against each other.

Just as hope was rising in his chest that they might slip out of camp unseen, the twin near the tree jerked his head up and opened his eyes. He blinked blearily as he tried to figure out what was going on, but it didn't take him long to figure out that he'd messed up. "Hey!" he shouted as he fiddled with the gun on his lap and tried to scramble to his feet. "Hey!"

This was enough to awaken the others. Trace was instantly sitting up, screaming orders as his cheeks reddened and spittle flew from his mouth. "What the fuck is wrong with you?" he yelled at the guard. "You had *one* job, motherfucker!"

"I've got them!" Eric was struggling to get his massive form out of his sleeping bag, which clung to him like a cocoon. He kicked and flailed until he finally flung it aside, lurching to his feet and grabbing that horrid whip.

Shiloh didn't have the same reservations about shifting that had run through Cash's mind as he woke up. She abandoned her job of severing the ropes. The scales that covered her clawed hands now rippled up her arms and across her shoulders. Her legs thickened, stretching the rope painfully against Cash's leg until it snapped. Her wings unfurled from her back, ripping through the back of her shirt with such force that Cash automatically jerked away. He was surprised to feel the buttery softness of the leather as it brushed against his arm. Stretching and popping to accommodate her dragon form, her neck and spine lengthened. Pain twisted her face for a moment as the Shiloh he knew disappeared and was replaced with a long muzzle and a head covered in spikes. Smoke rose from her nostrils as she swung her head about and searched for her first target.

Cash stared in disbelief. He'd been spending all

this time with Shiloh. He's experienced her dragon in abstract ways, feeling it reach out to his wolf as the two of them bonded the way the universe meant for them to whether they liked it or not. He'd seen merely a few scales on the back of her arm when she'd chosen to prove to him what she really was, even though she hadn't needed to. Though Cash had known exactly what beast lay under her human skin, he'd never imagined for a second that it would be so glorious. Her scales were a pale, pearly gold in indoor lighting. As the sunlight rose over the surrounding clifftops, however, it glinted off the shining metal armor she wore over her body. Cash was blinded not by the flash of those scales but by her magnificence as she dug her claws into the ground and stretched her wings out to their full glory.

If he hadn't already fallen for her, Cash would've gone tumbling over the edge just then. Shiloh was easily the most beautiful creature he'd ever seen in his life. She was massive and majestic. The sassy, funny woman he'd met in that little diner was now a bold and brazen dragon, a beast who wasn't willing to let anyone stand in the way of what she wanted.

Eric had managed to grab a whip. The brute was too stupid to fear the dragon in front of him, and he grinned as he activated the electrical charge by pressing a button on the handle. He pulled his arm behind him, prepared to whip Shiloh into submission the same way he'd done yesterday.

He'd underestimated this particular shifter. Shiloh's chest puffed out for a moment before her head shot forward on her neck, sending out a blast of flame that sizzled through the air and straight at his hand. Eric stubbornly held onto the weapon and threw his arm forward, intending to send the whip wrapping around Shiloh's long neck. The flame was stronger than he'd anticipated, burning the wooden handle to a crisp and sending an electrical shock straight up his own arm. Eric keeled backward, hitting the ground with a thud. His hand had spasmed into a tight fist, forcing him to keep a hold of the whip as it sent burst after burst of electricity through his body.

Finally getting a hold of himself, Cash looked to his left just in time to see the twin that'd been set as guard aiming that strange gun at Shiloh. He shot to his feet and shifted on the fly, his human feet leaving the ground as he ran and coming back down as paws. Cash dug into the ground for traction and put his head down as he barreled into the man, knocking him to the side and sending the gun flying.

Cash snatched it up in his teeth, ignoring the taste of metal in his mouth.

Tracy was still yelling commands, standing there next to the fire and pointing his finger. The remaining twin still hadn't managed to get on his feet and grab a weapon. Cash dodged to the right, heading for the boss of the operation, but Shiloh beat him to it. She whipped around to the side, sending her tail streaking through the remains of the campfire and straight into Tracy's legs. He flinched and put his hands out in front of him, a scream of terror escaping his throat, but there was nothing he could do to stop the pure force of her dragon energy. Shiloh sent him flying backward, tumbling against the ground.

Cash paused. The remaining twin simply stood there, jabbering with fear as his pants slowly turned wet. *Time to go!*

The wolf and dragon took off, streaking through the trees that grew on this side of the lake, and headed into the mountains. Cash listened, waiting for the sounds that would prove they were being pursued. His shoulders flinched in anticipation of gunfire, though it was obvious that this weapon he still carried in his mouth wasn't a typical firearm. He felt the thundering of the ground as Shiloh ran alongside him, but he looked at her when it suddenly stopped.

She was flying. She'd merely lifted her feet from the ground as she'd spread her wings, and the great dragon was soaring through the air. She kept her flight low so as not to make a target of herself, her steady wingbeats ruffling his fur as they put all their energy into their escape and headed around the curve in the path, leaving their captors behind.

18

SHILOH FELT HER WINGS GROWING TIRED, AND SHE SAW that Cash's wolf was starting to slow. She slowly descended to the ground next to him and folded her wings, running to absorb the impact before she slowed to a stop.

Cash pulled up next to her. She hadn't had much of a chance to look at his wolf before, but it was incredibly handsome. The thick ruff around his neck and the determined set to his eyes gave him a dignified look, like he was the wolf who ruled over this area. His fur was soft and plentiful in numerous shades of gray. It turned iridescent where it picked up the sunlight, making him far more of a beautiful creature than she'd ever known wolves could be. Shiloh studied him for a long moment, realizing that she'd never actually seen another person in their shifted form beside her aunt and—a long time ago—her parents.

He glanced over his shoulder, his pointed ears pricking in the direction they'd come from, but then he let his wolf fall away. His shift was smooth and efficient, and then Cash, the man, was standing in front of her once again.

Shiloh hesitated for a moment. She'd forgotten how comfortable she was in this skin. It made her feel strong, like she could take on the world. It was just what she'd needed as she'd tried to get comfortable in her human form in Sheridan, but of course, she couldn't show it off there. She felt a chill move in as her scales flipped and smoothed into the familiar form of her human body. Her ribs and spine crushed in as her wings folded back inside this new form, and for a moment, she felt like she couldn't breathe. Shiloh didn't panic. She expected this, and in just a couple of seconds, the feeling was gone.

"Are you all right?" Cash asked, walking slowly up to her and looking her over.

"I think so." Shiloh took stock of her body, finding that everything seemed to be intact. Shifters heal quickly to allow for quick form changes, and that probably didn't hurt. "It was all kind of a blur."

Cash nodded. "I know. I was hoping we'd be able to just sneak out of there so we could get a head start on them, but it didn't quite work out that way."

She smiled a little, realizing that she'd probably shifted far too early and far too fast. Not that she regretted it. There'd been something very satisfying about blasting that awful weapon right out of Eric's hand. "No, I guess not. Did you see the look on Tracy's face when I hit him?" she giggled.

Cash smiled. "I did. He's used to controlling people like us with his weapons, and I don't think he ever expected things to go wrong for him. Speaking of..." He picked up the gun he'd been carrying between his jaws and studied it.

"What do you think it is?" Shiloh asked, looking at it with both curiosity and a little fear. She too vividly remembered what it'd been like to be hit with that horrid whip, and she wasn't sure she wanted to know what this thing did. It looked similar to a regular gun, but there were wires that ran all over the outside and back into it.

He chewed his lip a little as he looked it over, frowning and shaking his head. "Interesting. It's essentially a sawed-off shotgun, but it doesn't use regular bullets. Look." He broke open the barrel and showed her the ammunition inside. “These are like miniature tasers.”

“Tasers?”

“It’s an electroshock weapon that uses electricity instead of bullets. Essentially, this weapon fires small projectiles that have electrified barbs on them. The back of the projectile is a battery, and I’d say all these extra weapons are to make sure they stay charged up. There’s even a chamber attached here for a few extra projectiles.”

Shiloh frowned. This was certainly not her area of expertise, but she thought she was understanding. “So this is just a gun version of those whips.”

“Yeah,” he said with a frown as he closed the barrel. “There was a hell of a lot of power in those things. Given that the hunters have figured out they can use it to revert the shift, I’m sure they’ve done something very similar here.”

“I don’t like the sound of that.” Shiloh rubbed her hand over her elbow, realizing just how lucky they were to have gotten away. If they hadn’t been awake before the others, and if their guard hadn’t fallen asleep the way he had, it wouldn’t have happened at all. Tracy and his cohorts had been cruel and determined when they’d captured Cash and Shiloh, and she had no doubt they would go to even greater lengths if they caught them again.

"No. I don't either. And I wish I had a better way of carrying this horrible thing, but since I don't have my backpack anymore, I'll just have to keep it in my hands. Or maybe I can tuck it in my waistband and hope it has some sort of safety." He frowned at it, and Shiloh guessed he was wondering how many other shifters it'd been used on.

Disgust for the thing filled her bones. "Why don't we just throw it in the lake? Or I can shift again and destroy it." Her chest grew hot just thinking about it, knowing the fire within her might not break down the gun's metal but that it would certainly melt the wires and render the weapon useless.

But Cash shook his head. "I'm keeping it, just in case. I can't say I'd mind a chance to turn around and use it on them. In the meantime, we'd better keep on pushing through."

Shiloh lifted her hands uselessly. "I don't have the map anymore. I don't know what they did with it when they found it in my backpack, and there wouldn't have been time to grab it, anyway." She frowned as she looked around, realizing that she had no idea where they were or where they should go.

"It's probably more important for us to just get back to your truck and into town."

"But think about how interested the hunters were in that map," Cash pointed out. "They're out here searching for something. They were looking for something in your cabin, which very well might've been the map itself. They were camped in an illegal spot not far from here. You said they showed up at your apartment. Whatever's going on, I don't think it's an accident. These men are here for a reason, and they think there's some sort of treasure to be found."

Shiloh's chest tightened. "If it's my map, and my cabin, then you'd think I'd know about it. Really though, Cash, Adelaide and I lived a pretty modest lifestyle. I can't imagine there would be any sort of treasure."

"But if there's something hidden in these mountains, do you want Tracy to get to it before you do?" he asked, his eyes hard with resolve.

"No, I suppose not." Shiloh looked around. "We don't have the map, though, so I doubt there's much we can do. I only know that we need to go up."

"So let's do it," Cash suggested. "At least we can give it a try, and if we don't find anything, then we'll at least know we tried."

"Okay."

They moved ahead on the trail, descending up along what seemed to be the path. It was growing much rougher as the elevation steadily increased, and large rocks and boulders dotted the grassy field on either side. Shiloh could feel her exhaustion as the path grew steeper. It wasn't an easy hike to begin with. Throw in a kidnapping and a restless night of being tied up, and the only thing that truly seemed appealing was to go home and go straight to bed.

But she also knew that Cash was right. They were already there, and there was obviously *some* reason that Adelaide wanted her to have that map. Thinking about finding the box under the floor reminded her that even though Tracy had taken that special piece of paper from her, he hadn't gotten everything. It was inconsequential, just a pendant that Adelaide had taken a liking to, but it felt good to know that all hadn't been lost.

They slowed as they crossed a stream. It was wide and shallow, rippling gently between the rocks that dotted it and served as stepping stones. It dropped down to the right, making a small waterfall, and Shiloh realized how thirsty she was. She paused to stick her hands in the cool rush of water.

Drink up, my dear, Adelaide's voice said. It was merely a memory, but it was a strong one. For an instant, Shiloh felt that she wasn't an adult out on a dangerous mission in the mountains but a little girl on a trip with her favorite aunt. *The water is good here, and we still have a long way to go.*

Shiloh shook the water from her hands, wondering what memories were getting mixed up inside her brain after all this time and all the life she'd lived just in the last few weeks. She and Adelaide used to go out hiking all the time. It was the best way to find good fishing spots or hidden berry bushes that would help supplement their pantry. Still, it felt as though she'd actually remembered that exact spot, which didn't seem likely.

The trail was now more of a climb. They scrambled up a short hill so covered in rocks that it hardly looked like a trail at all. Shiloh could see the summit far off in the distance, and she wondered if they were actually heading in the right direction. She'd hoped that some of the strange markings on the map would've given them some hint, but of course, they no longer had it.

When they made a switchback turn onto what was more obviously a trail, she didn't feel much better. Shiloh frowned to herself as she remembered how hard it had been to tell if the map was detailing the typical hiking trail or something else. She absently reached out and ran her hand along a sheer rockface on her right as she stepped over rocks and stones, trying to remember exactly what landmarks had been drawn on the map. There'd been something that sort of looked like a face, another that resembled a large lizard, and another that looked like claw marks. The only things she saw around her were rocks and grass, so what could those possibly mean?

She didn't know, but she once again heard Adelaide's voice as she lifted her hand from the rockface. *Just look at all these rocks. What do you think they are?*

Shiloh hadn't known. Weren't rocks just rocks?

Adelaide had laughed. *You look at them and see them for what they are, because that's all you've ever known them to be. Did you know that humans will see big rocks like this and decide they are giant monsters like dragons?*

We're monsters? Shiloh didn't sound like that little girl in real life anymore, yet she could hear it as though that little girl were walking alongside her right now.

No, my dear. We're not monsters, but it's important to know that some people think we are. Make sure you watch your step here, sweetie. The trail is a bit narrow.

With her memories superimposed over current events, Shiloh wasn't surprised at all to see the trail suddenly narrow as it fell steeply off to the right, revealing a breathtaking view of a massive gorge just before they reached the long, rugged ridgetop path that led to the summit.

"I've been here before."

Cash, who'd been moving doggedly along, stopped and turned around. "What?"

Shiloh paused and looked around. Just standing there didn't do anything to jog those old memories. It'd been the little things that had done it, and she didn't have a clue how to access another one. The fact remained that it'd happened, though, and that told her she had to be right. "I've been here before. It was a long time ago. I'd guess I was a little girl, and it would've been just after my parents died. Adelaide had gone out of her way to be extra nice to me at that point, and even as a kid, I knew she was doing it because she felt sorry for me." She smiled to herself as she remembered that distinct mix of sorrow and kindness in Adelaide's eyes as she'd put her arm around Shiloh and asked her if she'd gotten enough to eat.

"Why do you think you were here?" Cash asked. "Just a hike? Or something else?"

"I'm really not sure." Shiloh looked up to the peak, which seemed so close at this point even though she knew they still had some distance yet to go. "I know we came up this way, though. And we were on foot, because I remember putting my hands on the creek and coming up this part of the trail. I might not have been able to fly just yet."

"Interesting. I'm going to guess that means we're on the right track." He, too, glanced up at the peak, no doubt wondering if there was something up there.

"For the moment, I need to sit down and rest." Shiloh sank down on a nearby rock that was just the right height to make a seat, realizing all over again how tired she was. There'd been a burst of excitement as she'd experienced those old memories, but as soon as the adrenaline was gone, a wave of weakness followed. "I wish we still had all our camping supplies. Even if we find whatever we're looking for today, it's going to take a while to get back down the mountain."

Cash nodded as he sat across from her. The breeze rippled his hair, and a deep tan was setting in across his nose and cheeks. "That's true. I'd say we could shift to get back down, but flying would just make you a target."

Shiloh nodded. "I've thought about that. I've also thought I should've been a little more aggressive back there at the campsite. If I'd managed to kill them, then we wouldn't have anything to worry about. I just couldn't do it."

He reached forward and put a hand on her knee as he looked sincerely into her eyes. "Don't be so hard on yourself. Just because you're a dragon doesn't mean you're a monster."

"That's kind of you. Not everyone in the world thinks that way, though," she replied, once again going over that conversation with Adelaide in her mind.

A sound behind them made them both turn and look down the trail just in time to see Tracy, Eric, and the twins emerge around a bend in the path. Tracy's face was twisted in glee as he saw his prize sitting before him like a sitting duck. "Why do you look so stunned?" he asked, a cruel grin on his face. "Are you that surprised we could catch up with you? You're the ones who used up all that unnecessary energy on your escape plan this morning, especially when we were going to make you lead us to the treasure regardless."

Shiloh shot to her feet. "I don't have any damn

treasure!" she yelled. It was useless, but she was so angry. "Go rob a fucking bank if you're so broke!"

Tracy laughed, infuriating her even more. "As if that would be anything remotely close to the same thing. You know as well as I do that there are fortunes untold in this mountain. I've tracked down and killed dragons all over this country and even in a few others just to find it. I'm not about to give up when I'm this close."

Instinctively, Shiloh took a step backward. She stumbled over a rock and nearly fell, but Cash's strong hand caught her by the elbow and kept her on her feet. They exchanged a glance, and she had a feeling he was thinking the same thing she was. They were on a narrow, ridgetop path. There was nowhere to go, and the footing there was horrible. Since they were already outnumbered, and they only had the one electric gun in their arsenal, they had a distinct disadvantage.

Shiloh let go of the tension and fear that held her in her human body, pushing that energy into her shift. It hadn't been long since she'd been in her other form, and it was surprisingly refreshing to feel the warm sun on her neck as it lengthened. As they ruptured through her back and spread out, her wings picked up the slight breeze and reminded her of just how light her bones were in this form. Shiloh had no idea if her scales would be any sort of weapon against the electric bullets that she knew Tracy still had, but there was a certain amount of confidence that came from covering herself in her own natural armor. A shiver of pleasure rippled down her spine as she felt the spikes that covered her head, and her tongue fit just between her pointed teeth as she turned to Cash. “Hop on, cowboy.”

19

"WHAT?" CASH STARED AT THE GORGEOUS CREATURE in front of him. He wasn't surprised in the least that she'd shifted. Being on four feet on this ridge would be far safer than only two, and of course, she had wings to boot. There was always the risk that Tracy or his goons would shoot her out of the air with one of their fancy projectiles, but the ammo wouldn't feel good used against their human forms, either.

It didn't even shock him all that much to hear her speech. Shiloh hadn't spoken a word when they'd made their escape that morning, but no words were needed. She stood before him now, her amber eyes shining like glass as she watched him expectantly, her words sliding and hissing from her tongue like ice cubes in a hot pan.

"I said, get on," she repeated impatiently as she tried to keep an eye on both their would-be kidnappers and him. "We don't have a chance here. It's too close."

"Sure, but..." Cash gestured helplessly. Shiloh was standing there with the wing closest to him whipped forward and out of the way, giving him an easy path up to her back. He completely understood what she wanted, but even though she was the one insisting, it just didn't seem right. Shiloh wasn't a horse. She was a person, dragon or not.

Tracy was getting closer as he and his coterie progressed up the path and over the rocks. They could see just as well as Cash and Shiloh could that there was nowhere to go but to the summit. For the moment, they were too far out of range for the remaining electric whip. Cash guessed the guns required a relatively close range themselves, considering the weight of the cartridge. That didn't leave them much time before the hunters were upon them and they were out of options.

"Come on," Shiloh hissed in the odd dialog of an ancient creature. Her neck was arched backward and her chest was puffed out. Two slim lines of smoke escaped her nostrils as she prepared to fire upon the approaching brigands. "You're the one who said you were a rodeo star. This is as good of a time as ever to prove it."

"God damn it." She was right; he had no excuses. This wasn't the time to have a moral quandary. He kept himself facing the oncoming dragon hunters, just in case they didn't know he still had one of their guns tucked in the back of his waistband. He slipped in between Shiloh's wing and her giant, scaled body, feeling energy undulate through his fingertips as he touched her. This was different from touching her body when she'd brought him up to her apartment, yet it was just as intimate. He felt his face redden as he hoisted himself up onto her back.

Her shoulder blades and spine rolled under the cool scales as she backed up from the approaching hunters, and Cash noticed it felt very similar to riding a horse bareback. The biggest difference, however, was the fact that he had to spread his legs wider than he would on a mare or a gelding, and he didn't even have the advantage of a halter with a lead rope looped around it. Cash had seen fantasy movies where riders were perched just behind the dragon's head and could use the great spikes there to hold onto. Even though Shiloh was big, she wasn't big enough that he felt she could hold his weight out there on the end of her neck like that. The best he could do was to settle down between the spiny ridges on her back and tuck himself in behind her shoulder blades.

"We're out of time, so I hope you're ready."

When he was working the rodeo circuit and riding in team roping competitions, the cue to begin was always a short nod. Cash did this automatically, even though she couldn't see him. He felt her muscles tense as she bent her legs. With one huge thrust, Shiloh pushed against the ground. She shot up as her wings caught the air, whipping up a hurricane around his head. His stomach tried to stay on the ridgetop, falling straight down into his feet as they made their vertical ascent. It was just in time, as one of the taser bullets went flying past her legs and crashed against a boulder. Cash gritted his teeth against the sheer force of gravity as Shiloh banked first to the right and then to the left. She built up her elevation, but Cash noticed she wasn't just leaving the scene.

"You think we can do this?" he asked as he dared to pull the electric gun from his waistband. He hadn't ever used a weapon quite like this before, but it was easy enough to figure out. "Between your fire and this gun, I say we make sure these assholes never track you down again."

Shiloh swung around so that she could see the group on the ridgetop once again. Her wings swept through the crisp mountain air as she hovered for a moment. "It's going to be dangerous. There's no telling what sort of weapons they have, and you said the range was short on that gun. I'm willing if you are, though. I'm not going to live my life on the run."

Cash pumped the shotgun, loading one of the projectiles. "Let's go."

With an arching movement of her back, Shiloh dove down for Tracy's group. Cash's stomach was stuck to his spine. The biggest rollercoasters at the best theme parks had nothing on this ride as their bodies moved in unison. He kept his hips loose to adjust for her movements as his thighs clamped around her, and he watched the villains grow closer and closer through the sights along the barrel of the gun. There was nothing he wanted more than to give them a taste of their own medicine.

Shiloh's chest widened and her neck arched back as they approached, loading her own weapons. She swung from side to side, just to keep from giving them too easy of a target. She was getting closer to the ground now, but her wings beat furiously as she let gravity help her pick up speed.

His main target was Tracy, but he couldn't get a

good beat on him due to the angle. Cash adjusted his aim and fired, sending a miniature taser flying through the air just as Shiloh unleashed a ball of fire. The electrified bullet landed square in the middle of Eric's chest, making the big man stagger back slightly. He looked down at it, but he had no reaction at first to the thing clinging to him. Even Cash thought at first that perhaps it hadn't worked, because part of the projectile was now dangling from two wires. It activated, though, and Eric was soon tensing his arms and face in pain. He staggered backward into one of the twins, who stumbled and fell off the side of the ridgetop.

As they tilted and once again headed up into the sky, Cash understood why he hadn't been able to see Tracy. Shiloh had used him for her target. She'd hit her mark, and the man was screaming and slapping himself as he tried to put out the flames on his shirt.

"Nice," Cash said with a laugh.

"It's not enough, though," she returned, obviously not in the least bit amused by this adventure. "I'm going after him again."

A gunshot exploded through the air. Cash felt Shiloh lurch a little to the right.

"Fuck!" she exclaimed, the curse sounding odd

and frightening on her dragon tongue. "The little bastards think they can shoot us down!"

Cash's stomach dropped again, but this time it had nothing to do with altitude or speed. He saw the bleeding hole in Shiloh's wing. They had regular guns, after all. Anger flooded his system. He'd be damned if anyone tried to hurt her. She was still flying, and she hadn't lost any altitude, which was a good start. "Can they get through your scales with that?"

"I have no idea, but I guess we're going to find out. Are you ready?"

With another cartridge in the chamber, Cash looked down at the enemy. "More than ever."

He knew his focus this time as they once again came barreling out of the sky. Shiloh wanted Tracy's blood, and he couldn't blame her. The remaining twin was probably not a threat at all, considering how useless he'd been already, so Cash once again trained his eye on Eric. The bald man had ripped the electric bullet from his chest, and now he just looked like an angry elephant ready to go on a stampede. He held the other electrified shotgun, and Cash just had to hope that he had better aim than the goon.

As they descended, Cash noticed that Shiloh

wasn't summoning her fire as quickly as she had the last time. "I'm going in low," she called back to him. "This is it!"

He felt the determination through her body, and his own rose to meet it. They were going to do this. Cash leaned back to account for their steep incline, grateful for all his years in the saddle that had prepared him for this moment. He was just as resolved to finish this as she was, but as they swooped in low, he noticed that the surviving twin was the one with the gun. That meant they were going up against both regular bullets and electric ones, and he spotted at the last moment that Tracy had the remaining whip in his hand.

The twin, angry and shaking from the loss of his brother, fired first. The bullet went straight between Shiloh's wings. Cash felt his wolf taking control, keeping him calm and steady as he aimed and fired once again at Eric. This time, the bullet hit him right in the forehead.

Shiloh was even with the ground now as she raced along the ridgetop and right at Tracy. He held the whip at the ready. Half of his face was burned, making him look like some gruesome monster, but still, he grinned. Shiloh blasted him with another ball of fire as she skimmed the ground. Her jaws, already open to allow for the fire, snapped around Tracy's head at the last moment. Blood exploded into the air and splattered on her golden scales as she came in for a rough landing.

Cash pulled up his legs and rolled off her back, shifting in midstride and leaving the shotgun behind. In wolf form, he no longer cared at all if the remaining goon shot him. The only thing that was important was that he killed them all, and his vision was red with fury as he bounded straight at the twin. His teeth clamped around the man's throat, and the gun dropped uselessly to the ground as Cash stripped him of his lifeblood, shaking him like a rag until he went limp. Turning, Cash was ready to take on Eric, who lay on the ground with the taser sticking out of his forehead. The wires that extended when the battery deployed on impact were singed, and so was the skin around the prongs that had burrowed into him. The taser had malfunctioned and sent a deadly electrical charge instead of a disabling one, and his soul had left his body.

It was done.

20

SHILOH WAS STILL SHAKING AS SHE SCRUBBED HER SKIN in the cold, clear water of a creek. Her clothes were soaking wet, but she didn't care. The amount of flame she'd summoned had left her too warm, and after that mountaintop battle, she just wanted to be clean.

"You really think it'll be okay?" she asked as Cash stood from his place next to her in the stream.

He hadn't thrown his entire body into the shallow water the same way she had, but he'd stripped off his shirt. Water glistened on his toned chest and shoulders and dripped from his hair as he sat back on a nearby rock. "Yeah. The bodies are hidden, and your fire burned away any hint of blood. At the very most, someone might think an errant hiker had started a campfire up here and lost control."

Shiloh nodded. She'd been horrified when she'd realized the impact of what they'd done, even though she knew that Tracy and his cohorts had deserved it. They were dragon hunters. They wouldn't have stopped until she was dead, so she had no reason to feel otherwise about them. Still, it had made her heart freeze to realize that she'd been responsible for the end of someone's life. Cash had assured her that shifter issues often had to be covered up for the greater good of their kind, and that sometimes included hiding incidents like this.

Standing up, she flicked her hands through the air to dry them before she removed the piece of paper from her pocket. She'd managed to retrieve it from Tracy's things, and it felt strange to hold the map again. "If you're still up for it, I think I've got this map figured out now."

Cash's head shot up in surprise. "You do?" he laughed.

"What's so funny?" she demanded, feeling defensive.

He shrugged and smiled. "Just that we've spent the past day and a half being kidnapped, escaping, climbing a mountain, and then killing our captors, but all of a sudden, you've managed to solve the puzzle of an old map?"

"If you're done, you don't have to come with me."

He tipped his head to the side and gave her a stern look. "Don't be like that. Of course, I'll come with you."

Somewhere deep inside, she knew she was struggling. She'd been through a lot over the last couple of days, and even over the last few weeks. The pregnancy test results shot to the forefront of her mind then, and that was enough to stress out over without being taken captive and killing a man with her own teeth. The last thing she wanted to do was to be oversensitive, but it was difficult to shove it down. "I saw some things while we were in the air," she explained, closing her eyes to help regain those images. "As focused as I was on taking the hunters out, I couldn't help but notice certain rock formations. I don't think the map was intended to be followed on foot."

"Oh?" Cash stood and came around next to her to look at the map.

The bare skin of his chest and arms was mere inches from her, and Shiloh felt her body reacting. She swallowed and reminded her dragon that it'd done enough for the day, thank you very much. "The trail is almost identical to the common one that hikers use all the time. But you see these symbols? The lizard and the face? You can only see them from the air. They're created from the lower mountains that surround Cloud Peak. The claw marks, over here right next to the X, are just down off the trail and to the east. Whatever this map is leading us to isn't far from here."

Cash nodded as he studied the map. "We're all the way up here. I'm up for checking it out if you are."

Shiloh couldn't remember ever being so exhausted in her life. Perhaps when she'd first received the news of her parents' deaths and had done nothing but sleep next to Adelaide for several days, but that had been a different kind of fatigue than what was brought on by fighting for her survival. Still, it wasn't as though she could go back to normal without settling the mystery of the map. "Sure."

She didn't need to take to the air again to find the place where they were going. As she led the way across a nearby ridgetop, she was glad. Shiloh had shifted into her dragon form far too much recently, and she had to wonder how Cash felt about it. He'd known she was a dragon, and it wasn't as though he didn't have an animal inside himself as well. Still, she had to wonder if perhaps it'd been too much for him. He didn't know any other dragons, so it had to be an odd experience.

Guilt weighed heavily on her mind as she once again replayed the scene of the battle. In the heat of the moment, she'd been thirsty for Tracy's blood. Now that it was over, she wondered if she'd gone too far. Should she simply have flown away? The logical part of her brain told her that killing him was the right thing to do, but it was hard for her to accept when she could still taste the hunter's blood on her tongue.

"I think this is it," she said when she spotted thc three small valleys that would make the claw mark from the air. She moved down from the ridgetop to investigate, but everything just looked like more of the endless rocks they'd been climbing through ever since they'd left the grassy foothills. The sun beat down on her head and her stomach rumbled, and she started to wonder if she could possibly go any further.

Cash was next to her again. "Do you know if you were here before?" he asked quietly, "when you came up here with your aunt?"

Her brain felt like mush in her head, and Shiloh

thought she might cry. It wasn't fair to come all this way for nothing, and no memories had come rushing back to her. Surely, if there were something important enough to require a map, and important enough that it should be passed down to her, then she would remember it. "I don't think so. I don't remember this area at all. It was such a long time ago. I just..." She trailed off as something caught her eye.

Shiloh stepped forward, deep into one of the recesses. She trailed her finger on the rockface, noticing the pattern etched into the stone. It was a small filigree engraving, and she knew she'd seen it before. Shiloh pulled the key out from underneath her shirt. There was no place to insert the key, as one would if they were unlocking a house or a padlock, but she pressed the decorated top of it against the etching. It matched perfectly, and she heard something click deep in the mountain.

In front of her, the rock rolled away to reveal a huge gap in the shadows of the ravine. It was dusty and dark, but her heart lifted. The scene before her wasn't familiar, but the rumbling sound of stone sliding against stone was a familiar one. *Stay right here, child, and I'll be back in just a moment. Then we'll be on our way home again.* Adelaide had brought her along, but she hadn't taken a young Shiloh into the mountain itself.

The opening was just big enough to bend over and look into, but Shiloh could see nothing. She gripped the newly discovered doorway to back out, but her hand had landed on a switch of some sort. A flame burst into life on her right, followed by another one next to it, and then another as torches lit up along the walls of a vast cave.

"Oh my god." Shiloh stepped all the way inside, finding a shallow set of stairs that led downward and allowed her to stand all the way. She was in a vast underground room, one that was filled with chests, boxes, and barrels. Dust coated every surface and filled the air.

"Holy shit." Cash had followed her inside, but he hovered just behind her. He leaned over and peeked into one of the chests, and Shiloh caught a glimpse of gold coins. "I guess Tracy was right about treasure, after all."

"I—I guess so," Shiloh stammered, hardly knowing how to process this. She simply stood there at the bottom of the stairs, letting her eyes adjust to the light and trying to understand. She lifted a bag that sat on top of a barrel. It was small and delicate, and when she poured it out, her hand was filled with diamonds. "Adelaide never told me about this. I do think she came here when we went out on our hike all those years ago, but I'd say she only took what she needed to make sure she could care for a child. We never had a lot of money, so I'm guessing she didn't ever come back."

"I'd say at least someone did at some point," Cash said quietly, pointing to the floor.

A set of footprints headed into the cave and back out, but they'd already started filling back in with dust. Shiloh followed them to the back of the room, where a torch in the shape of a dragon's head breathed flame over a small table. A small box sat on top of that table, one that was very similar to the carved container Shiloh had found under the floor-board of the cabin. With shaking fingers, she opened it and found yet another note. Her throat was thick. Her eyes burned with tears or dust, or maybe both, but she slowly unfolded it.

My dearest Shiloh,

If you've found this place, then I do hope the riches it contains may help you forgive me for not telling you about it sooner. The legends about our kind are some-what true, and we do like to keep our hoard a secret. I'd never have chosen to keep it from you at all, save that knowledge of it can be a great burden. This place contains all the wealth that our clan accumulated over the centuries. We've been careful with it, each one of us adding something of ourselves as our lives come and go. You are the last one for now, but I hope that your future generations will continue the tradition.

SHILOH CHOKED ON HER TEARS. SHE PRESSED HER hand to her mouth and then to her stomach. Even in death, Adelaide had managed to remind her of her responsibility to the future.

SPEAKING OF WELL-KEPT SECRETS, THERE IS ANOTHER ONE that I must finally tell you. Again, please forgive an old dragon, one who couldn't bring herself to see the face of her beloved niece—someone whom she thought of as a daughter—and so waited until she was dead to share this dreadful truth. I've already cautioned you on those who would seek our elimination. Dragon hunters have existed almost as long as dragons have. That they exist is no mystery. But I must tell you now, my dear child, that your parents didn't perish in an accident while they were on vacation. Hunters killed them, slaying them simply because of who and what they were. I didn't want you to grow up in fear, so I spared you that information. I'm sorry for that, but I'm not sorry for seeing the way you smiled and the light in your eyes when we shared time together.

I love you, Shiloh. I do hope that you're safe and well, and that you'll find the life you crave for yourself now that I'm gone.

Adelaide

"ARE YOU ALL RIGHT?" CASH ASKED SOFTLY, STILL lingering respectfully in the doorway.

Shiloh put the note back in the box, thinking it was just as much of a treasure as the rest of the items in there. "Not really, but I will be."

"What are you going to do with all of this?"

She sighed. There was no telling what was in these containers, but it was undoubtedly valuable considering the small part of it that she'd already seen. There was enough wealth that she'd never have to work again in her life if she didn't want to, but as Adelaide's note pointed out, that wasn't the type of life she was looking for. She returned to the small bag of diamonds and slipped one in her pocket. She felt almost guilty, but she knew it would provide for the little one she had on the way. Adelaide would've wanted that, she knew.

"Is that all you're going to take?" Cash asked. "With everything you've got here, you can afford to be as independent as you want to be."

His words made her spine stiffen. Shiloh didn't dare to look at him, because that last sentence told her everything she needed to know. She'd spoken too much to him about wanting to be unfettered by the close company of a man, and all while she'd relied on him heavily. Shiloh had managed to show him too much truth about herself, even as she learned it. She couldn't blame him for losing interest. He was a good man, one who'd risked his own life to save hers, but she came with far too much baggage.

"This is all I need for now." Shiloh felt the sharp point of the diamond dig into her skin as she went back up the stairs and out into the sunshine.

21

"Cash? Cash. Deputy Taylor!"

Cash blinked and looked up to find Eve standing over his desk, a look of concern on her face as she pushed several slips of paper at him. "You've gotten several phone calls in. I took messages because I'd thought you'd left on patrol an hour ago," she said pointedly.

"Right. Thanks." Cash took the papers, but he barely skimmed them before he set them near his computer. "I was researching this case, and I got a little distracted."

"I see. Um..." Eve looked toward Levi's office. He wasn't in at the moment, but her worries were written all over her face. "I know you'd like to get that robbery figured out, but you may want to make sure you get your regular duties covered, too."

Irritation wrinkled Cash's forehead. He knew Eve meant well. She mothered the entire department in her sweet, modest way. She was like the mom from one of those old fifties sitcoms, who tried to gently guide without stepping on anyone's feet. Still, he had work to do, and he didn't need her hovering over him and correcting him like a schoolboy. "There's a lot of surveillance footage to go over here. I can't just walk away from that."

Eve pressed her lips together and took a breath. She turned slightly as though she would walk away, but then she shook her head at herself and squared herself up in front of Cash. "Look, I won't pretend to know exactly what's going on with you, but I'd suggest you fix it."

He leaned back in his chair, surprised to hear her talk like that. It was far more direct than he was used to. "Fix what?"

She gestured helplessly at his desk, which was completely covered in files and papers. "Whatever it is you've got going on that has you so involved in some random robbery that you're not doing your job. No one likes going out on patrol. It's boring, and I'm sure every other deputy here would much rather feel like they're making a bigger difference than helping old ladies who've locked themselves out of their cars or catching some young kid who's speeding through town. But those same deputies are starting to talk, and it isn't exactly a secret that Levi has already talked to you several times. I'm just telling you that if you keep going down this path, you're going to find yourself without a job. It's up to you if you decide to do anything about it." Her lips trembled slightly as she finished, and Cash had the feeling it'd taken a lot out of her just to say that.

He nodded slowly, seeing exactly what she meant. Ever since he'd met Shiloh, he'd swung back and forth from one end of the spectrum to the other, either throwing himself so completely in his work that he had no personal life or barely even getting through a shift. He still hadn't managed to find the sense of balance he'd wanted, and maybe it had gotten even worse. Eve's admonishment irked him, but she was just trying to keep him from getting in trouble again. "You're right. I've just been going through some things. I'll work on it."

She gave a nod and took a step back. "You know, I'm always happy to help in any way I can."

"Thanks, Eve."

She returned to her desk, and Cash wanted to

kick himself. He knew he deserved it. No grown man should let himself get so distracted by a woman, especially one who didn't want him. Shiloh had told him from the very beginning that she didn't want a relationship, and Cash had thought he could wait her out. Once they'd shared that long and dangerous hike up to Cloud Peak, he'd still held some hope that she would see the fated connection between them, the bond that had brought them together against all odds. In the end, though, they'd parted ways when they'd come back down from the Big Horns without a word spoken about any potential for a future together.

Cash went through the motions of the day, feeling like he wasn't even in his own body as he patrolled Sheridan. It was someone else who sat near the intersection and waited until a truck rolled through a red light. It was someone else who answered the call on the radio and showed up to help settle a domestic dispute, which turned out to be little more than a young couple arguing over money and ended peacefully. It was still someone else who turned in the paperwork, because Cash himself was just watching it all as though it were a dream.

When his shift was over, he thought he could

shake off this cold feeling of distance and disinterest as he headed over to the Full Moon Saloon. He nodded at Shaw behind the bar, but he didn't stop for a beer. Instead, he threaded through the crowd and all the way to the back of the room to a narrow set of stairs that led to the second level. It was time for the monthly pack meeting, and even though Cash normally dreaded these affairs, he was eager for some sort of distraction. Work just wasn't cutting it.

He sat near the front of the room where he could watch the other members drift in. Some of them he couldn't recall seeing in the last several months, which told him just how much distance he'd put between himself and his pack. Cash only felt more lost.

Colton stepped into the room with a beer in his hand and sat down across from Cash. Bryce, a ranch hand who worked for Colton, settled in next to him. "You're here," Colton called out.

"Shouldn't I be?" Cash challenged, feeling defensive. Just because he hadn't been coming to the meetings for a while didn't mean he was any less of a member.

The rancher eyed him curiously. "Sure. I just figured you'd be working or something. That's what usually happens on meeting nights. It's not always easy to tear yourself away from the demands of life to come."

Bryce lounged against the table, twisting his beer bottle in his hand and looking for any sexy young wolves. "I can't say I'd mind being somewhere else myself. I was supposed to have a hot date tonight."

"Pfft." Colton slugged him in the arm. "No, you didn't. You told me you didn't have anything better to do."

"Right, because she had to go see her grandma in the hospital," Bryce replied, looking pissed as he took a sip of his beer and ran a hand through his thick, dark hair.

His boss shook his head. "Dude, that's what girls say when they've decided they don't want to go out with you anymore and they don't want to hurt your feelings."

Bryce shook his head and took another slug of beer. "Maybe they say that to you, but not to me. Trust me, she was interested."

Colton laughed. "Sure she was."

"Right, because you know so damn much and you're so much better than everyone else. Pardon me for forgetting." Bryce shoved himself up from his seat and headed across the room to a different table.

"Don't mind him," Colton advised, thumbing over his shoulder at his employee. "He's just crabby because he hasn't gotten laid in a while. What about you? Is that what your problem is?"

Cash sighed. He'd always known Colton to be bold, sometimes to the point of rudeness. "I'm fine, but thanks so much for your interest," he replied sarcastically.

He was saved from having to dive any further into that discussion by the arrival of Shaw, who'd left one of his employees in charge of the bar while he came upstairs to run the meeting. He glared around the room with his scarred eye, waiting for everyone to be quiet before he started. "I thank you all for coming," he said in that quiet monotone voice of his that always permeated a room. "It seems we have more than we normally do, which is good since we have much work to be done."

Cash's mind wandered as Shaw went over the discussions from the previous meeting. He hadn't seen Shiloh in over a week, yet he could still see her warm eyes looking at him with gratitude when he'd offered to go with her to Cloud Peak. Then there was the everlasting image of her as a gorgeous, ferocious dragon, fighting off those who sought to hurt them. It didn't matter what form she was in or what she was doing. He just wanted to be with her again. So many times, he'd considered stopping at her apartment or heading to Cowpunch Coffee, but he knew he'd only be turned down.

"And so, I need someone to volunteer to go over the account books and find the discrepancy," Shaw was saying when Cash came back to the present moment.

He lifted his hand. "I'll do it."

Shaw raised an eyebrow, but nodded. "Thank you. And I need someone to help Mr. and Mrs. Wright move out of their home and into their new apartment."

Cash vaguely remembered him saying something about the older couple needing to find a place that was more manageable for them in their older age. The pack always helped their own. He raised his hand again.

Shaw made a note of it, along with a few other men and women who'd volunteered. "As our numbers have grown, we've discussed building a new place to have our meetings. I'm happy to donate the property, but this is something that will take a lot of hard work."

Cash had his hand in the air before Shaw could even ask for specific needs. He didn't care what the work was or how hard it was. He just needed something to keep him from going home at night and staring blankly at the television while he thought about Shiloh.

When the meeting concluded, he stood to head downstairs with the others. Cash felt the heavy weight of Shaw's gaze on him, though, and the older man nodded toward the back of the room. Shit. Shaw wasn't a man of many words, and it couldn't be good if he wanted to talk to him.

A small bar sat in the very back of the long, second-story room. Shaw fell into the same role he served downstairs as he poured two shots of whiskey. His mouth was a hard line as he watched the amber liquid roll into the glasses, but his eyes were kind as he looked up at Cash. "What's going on?"

Once again, Cash felt his hackles raise in defense. Why was everyone attacking him tonight? "What do you mean?"

Shaw scratched his face, rubbing his fingers over the scar that had devastated it many years ago. "You don't earn the position of Alpha by being unobservant. You've hardly volunteered for a single thing in the past, but tonight you couldn't keep your hand down. I'd suggest you tell me."

Cash considered lying. It was easier than admitting the truth. A grown man could finally decide he wants to serve his pack in the best way possible, right? Shaw would know, though. The man knew everything. "It's about this woman..."

"The dragon?" Shaw asked quietly before knocking back his drink.

Cash felt his mouth fall open. It wasn't a shock that the older man knew who he was talking about, since he'd seen Cash and Shiloh talking right there in his bar. If Shaw knew the truth about her, then the Alpha really did pay attention to things around him.

"That's the one," he confirmed. "We went on one date, and it was fantastic. I couldn't believe it when she said she didn't want to see me anymore. I can feel the bond between us. You know the one I'm talking about." Old shifter legends about fate and destiny were still in wide circulation, and plenty of shifters still felt that connection hit them when they met their mates.

Shaw poured another round of drinks. "Ah, so you believe the two of you are supposed to be together, and you don't think she feels the same." It wasn't a question.

"Right." Cash sighed. He was used to typical

locker-room talk when it came to women, but it just wasn't like that with Shaw. The bartender had a soft spot for women, and he wouldn't tolerate even the slightest bit of filthy talk from any of his pack members. Somehow, it was much harder to talk about the real stuff. "She says she wants to find herself, but then she still wanted my help. Shaw, we went up into the mountains and slayed a group of dragon hunters, for fuck's sake. I've done everything I can for her, and I hardly get more than a thank you. I just don't understand how she can walk away from something like that."

Shaw tipped his glass back and moved his tongue over his teeth, tasting the fineness of the whiskey as he turned the empty glass in his hands. "Did you ask her?"

"Why should I? She already told me she didn't want to see me anymore, at least not like that." Frustration was building in Cash once again.

"But that was before everything else happened?"

"Yeah." Cash rubbed his hands over his face as he recalled every shy glance, every curious look, and even the way she'd held his hand throughout the night.

"If you haven't talked to her about it, then I don't know why you're here. Go to her. Tell her. Tell her everything. Not just that you feel for her, but exactly *what* you feel for her. You're withering away because of what you *think* she wants when you haven't even bothered to ask," Shaw advised.

"I guess so."

"I know so," Shaw replied firmly, setting his glass down with a clink and looking Cash square in the eye. "Women aren't like us. They're much smarter, but they're just as insecure. Go to her. Throw yourself at her feet and upon her mercy. Give her the chance to tell you to her face what she wants from you."

"And if she still isn't interested?" Cash pressed.

Shaw stuck his lower lip out slightly with a shrug. "Then she'll have decided your fate, and you'll have to deal with it."

22

"There you are. Let me know if you need anything else." Shiloh set the plates in front of her customers and turned to head back to the kitchen.

"Uh, Miss?"

"Hm?" She turned around, feeling like she was living in an endless nightmare of waiting tables and constantly getting orders wrong. No one bothered her when she did things right, after all.

"I ordered a tuna melt, not a hamburger." The older man—a truck driver, she thought—was at least kind enough to correct her politely instead of yelling at her.

"I'm sorry. I'll have the tuna melt right out to you." Shiloh scooped up the plate with the hamburger and hurried back to the kitchen, wondering if there was anyone who'd actually ordered the burger or if she'd just completely botched it. "Bennie, can you whip me up a tuna melt really quick? I screwed up again."

The cook nodded and went to work while Shiloh headed to the drinks station. Someone had ordered a Coke, hadn't they?

"Shiloh, honey." Barb had just come out of her office, and Shiloh realized that her boss had seen the whole thing. "Can I talk to you for a second?"

Disappointment flooded over her. She didn't want to let Barb down. The woman had been so kind to her, even when she didn't have to be. "I've just got to get these drinks out."

Barb took the pitcher of tea out of Shiloh's hand and set it down. "It can wait for a moment, I think. I'm worried about you, dear. Your body is here, but your mind isn't. I don't blame you, since I know what you've got going on, but you're just not yourself."

"I know." Shiloh swallowed. The truth was that she'd done nothing but think of Cash ever since they'd come back to town. She'd had so much to think about, but Cash's silence and distance had been the heaviest on her mind. Shiloh knew she'd made a mistake when she'd told him she didn't want to get into a relationship with him. He'd proven that to her over and over again with how much he was willing to do for her. But how could she just turn around and tell him what an idiot she was?

Barb took Shiloh's hands and sandwiched them between her own. "Have you been to a doctor or anything?"

Shiloh shook her head. There was no telling what the child growing inside her would turn out to be. Was it a dragon? A wolf? Would it look like a normal human baby to a doctor?

"Then that's one thing we need to get lined up," Barb said, speaking as though she were making a mental checklist of everything that needed to happen. "Now, then. How about the father?"

Words completely escaped her every time she even thought about telling Cash. Shiloh had no good reason to believe he'd be upset. He'd been part of the act that had made this child, after all. He'd been willing to drive her up to her cabin, hike up a mountain, and even to help kill those who threatened her. He'd stayed at her side through all of that, yet panic bloomed in her chest every time she envisioned what it would be like to let the words come out of her mouth and to his ears. This wasn't a commitment of a day or a weekend. This was an entire life. "What about him?" she strangled out.

Barb tipped her chin down and looked up at Shiloh. "Don't tell me you haven't told him."

"I don't have to." Shiloh lifted her head, trying to make herself look braver than she felt. She was terrified. Adelaide had done a good job of keeping her from living a life of fear, but now dread filled every second of her life. How could she tell Cash? How could she not? What would it be like to raise a baby, especially when it wasn't as though she had anyone around to help her? Sure, she had Alexis, but her friend didn't exactly seem like the motherly type. Barb was, but Shiloh couldn't expect that kind of responsibility from her boss. Shiloh had grown up almost alone, and her child would have a similar existence. "I can do this on my own."

The older woman shook her head. "That's crazy. No one can do this on their own, and they shouldn't have to. At least give him the chance to do the right thing. If he doesn't, well then, that's on him. He should, though."

"Maybe." Shiloh knew Barb meant that Cash should help financially. The funny thing was, Shiloh didn't need any help when it came to money. A mere flight up to Cloud Peak would give her all the financial security she could possibly need. To her, though, it wasn't about that. Sure, a baby would be expensive. She might have lived a life of isolation, but she did know that much. She wasn't afraid of how she would buy diapers or formula.

"There's no maybe about it. You need to tell him. I understand if you think you want to do this alone. Men can be a real pain in the ass. But you can't just wait tables until you pop," Barb warned.

"I guess that's true," Shiloh admitted. This was exactly what she didn't want, but she didn't know how to avoid it. She'd longed to find a life for herself, to figure out who she was and what she wanted. All these fantasies about exploring Sheridan and then maybe even going off to a big city someday had come crashing down around her. Even the potential of getting back together with Cash seemed threatened by the presence of the baby, yet her responsibility to her child meant more than anything. Not for the first time that day, tears pricked her eyes. It seemed all she did anymore was cry. "It just seems so unfair. It's like the rest of the world is deciding my fate instead of me."

"Oh, honey." Barb pulled her into her arms and stroked the back of her hair as she swayed slightly. "I'm sorry to tell you, but that's just how life is. We can have all the best intentions, but we don't always get to see them through. I like to think it's destiny's way of telling us that it knows better than we do when it comes to what's good for us, and we have to learn to accept that sometimes."

Shiloh sniffled as she nodded, pulling away and finding a paper napkin to wipe her nose. "It's going to be hard."

"I know, honey. You can do it. And like I said before, I'm here for you. You don't *have* to do any of this alone. I think it's important to know that, so you'll probably hear me harping on it a lot." Barb chuckled a little to herself as she looked into Shiloh's face. "Do you still want to finish this shift, or do you need to go home?"

Shiloh shook her head against the notion of going home. She'd loved her apartment when she'd first rented it, even when she hardly had enough furniture to fill one room and was still busting her ass to get it all painted. Now, though, it felt more like a prison cell than anything else. It was a place for her to wander from one corner to another, trying not to think about where she would put a crib and if this was even a good neighborhood to raise a family. When her feet grew tired, she'd just lay on the couch and think of Cash, wondering if he thought about her at all or if she'd just been another wild adventure for him.

"I want to work," she replied solidly. "I can't just sit around and do nothing."

"But you'll do some of the other things we talked about?" Barb asked.

Her stomach lurched, but she nodded once again. "Yeah. I will."

"Okay. In that case, your tuna melt is ready. Get that out there, but let me know if you need any extra breaks."

Shiloh did her best to throw herself into her work, pushing away all thoughts of Cash, the baby, and even Adelaide from her mind. Cowpunch Coffee was one place where she didn't have to worry about being a mother or a partner or a niece. She was simply a waitress, and she would do her damnedest to be the best one in Sheridan. "Here's your tuna melt, sir. Thank you for your patience. Let me know if you need anything else."

23

"There you go. I think that's the last of it," Cash said as he set down a box on the dining table in Mr. and Mrs. Wright's new apartment. His back ached from all the heavy lifting, and he was pretty sure his toe was going to be black the next morning after he'd dropped one end of the upright piano on it, but he didn't mind. He'd volunteered to help the older couple, and it had been a welcome distraction. It wasn't his typical routine at work, and he was grateful to have the day off so he could avoid Levi for a bit longer. Neither was moping around at his place, thinking about Shiloh and trying to decide whether or not he should be following Shaw's advice.

"Thank you so very much." Mrs. Wright, a frail woman with ghostly white hair and dark eyes, patted him on the shoulder and smiled at him as though he were her own son. "It's been so nice to have all of you here, but even more so to see you."

"Me?" Cash glanced over his shoulder, seeing that the other men who'd offered to help were sitting on the front porch with Mr. Wright, who'd just arrived with a large case of beer as a thank you.

"Certainly!" She pulled out a dining chair and sat, exhausted from a day of deciding where the sofa should go and fussing over whether or not their furniture was too heavy for the men to lift. "You work for the sheriff's department, right? I think it means a lot that an officer of the law also cares about his community. Not everyone is that way these days, you know."

A flush crept over his cheeks as he looked at the carpet at his feet. "I don't know. I like to think any of the other deputies would do the same thing."

"Well, it still means a lot to me. Now, with you having such a good job and such a handsome face, why don't you tell me why you're so sad?"

Cash jerked his head up. "I'm not sad."

Mrs. Wright was almost ninety years old, but she still managed to give him a rather stern look. "Don't pretend with me. I see the way you are, looking wistfully at everything around you as though you can't quite be a part of it. Why, you'd be out there with the other men right now having a beer if you thought you could handle it."

He glanced over his shoulder out the front window, and he knew Mrs. Wright had spoken the truth. He'd helped with the move because he wanted a diversion, but it hadn't worked completely. He'd seen the photos of Mr. and Mrs. Wright propped up on the mantel, displaying decades of married bliss. His heart had ached when he saw the soft look in Mr. Wright's eyes as he checked on his wife to make sure she wasn't overworking herself. The two of them had something that seemed so special, yet he knew that it wasn't anything he could ever have for himself. On the complete opposite end of the spectrum, he'd heard the other young men of the pack laughing and joking about women they'd dated or that they'd wanted to date. It all left Cash feeling as though he were floating in limbo with no direction.

"You're right," he finally admitted. "I just have some things I'm working through."

"Heartbreak?" she pressed.

"Yeah. Yeah, I guess that is what you'd call it." Putting a name on it made it even harder to swallow.

Mrs. Wright nodded knowingly. "I've already nosed my way into your business too much, but do yourself a favor. If you have anything you think you still need to say to her, then do it. Even if you don't think it's going to make the tiniest bit of difference, do it anyway. My Jim thought our relationship was over way back when we were teenagers because my parents didn't approve of him. He showed up at our house, though, and he spilled his whole heart on the floor. It wasn't easy for him, but it let my parents know that our feelings for each other were real and not just puppy love. Jim didn't give up, and neither should you."

Mrs. Wright's advice echoed in his head for the rest of the afternoon as he headed to the grocery store, stopped for gas, paid the water bill, and went home to put the groceries away. Was he giving up? When was it the right time to give up? He really didn't know. *Even if you don't think it's going to make the tiniest bit of difference,* Mrs. Wright had said. Well, he wasn't sure it would. Cash couldn't think of any grander gesture to show his love than the ones he'd already made, but that could very well be the problem. Maybe it didn't take a grand gesture.

He got back in his truck and pulled out of the driveway, drumming his thumbs on the steering wheel and wondering how much of a mistake this all was. Shiloh was the kind of person who would at least listen to him. He was fairly certain of that. Even with all the emotional events that she'd been through over the last few weeks as she discovered that hunters were out to kill her and steal her family fortune, and as she'd learned the truth about her parents' deaths, she will still also the kind of person who knew exactly what she wanted. The kind of determination it takes to plunge ahead even when you're exhausted and starving is exactly what he would've expected from her, and he had no doubt that it boded poorly for any results he might have.

Still, as though he had no actual control over his body, Cash guided the car toward Cowpunch Coffee. The inertia of his mission could no longer be avoided. Everyone else seemed to think he should be doing this. Wade had advised him to stay in Shiloh's life. Shaw had told him to throw himself at her feet. Even old Mrs. Wright had encouraged him to open his heart and give her the chance to hear everything he had inside it before he walked away for good.

The diner wasn't busy when he pulled up in front. Cash didn't know if that was a good or a bad thing. An empty dining room would mean fewer people to stare at him, but it would also be far too quiet. It didn't matter now. He'd already parked, and anyone inside would've seen his truck. If Shiloh was one of them, and she saw him chicken out and hit reverse, then she'd probably never even give him a chance. He got out and headed inside.

Barb was at the counter, ringing up a customer and chattering loudly about how nice the weather was and how good the apple pie was that day. She eyed him only long enough to see that a new customer was coming in.

Cash took his usual table near the back. This was the same place where he'd sat with Levi and where he'd met Shiloh for the first time. He'd been there when she'd asked him to go on that fateful trip to her cabin, a drive that would lead to an even bigger escapade that would leave their lives hanging in the balance. And so it only seemed fitting that he would sit there once again as he took this final step. If she was there, then it was now or never.

Only a minute later, Shiloh emerged from the kitchen. Cash watched as she stopped to check on a customer near the front windows, smiling and laughing with him as she asked if he wanted dessert. She turned toward the counter, where Barb nodded her head in Cash's direction.

As soon as her eyes met his, the smile melted from her face. Shiloh stood frozen in the middle of the diner, simply staring at him. She brought her hands up, twisting her fingers in front of her apron as she decided what to do. With a lift of her chin and a purposeful step, she crossed the room toward him. Instead of stopping at the side of his table to ask for his order, though, she sat across from him.

"We need to talk," they both said at the same time.

Cash laughed a little, feeling relieved that she wasn't just sticking to doing her job and dismissing him as though he were any other customer. "Ladies first."

"So gallant of you." A hint of the twinkle he'd first noticed was in her eyes, but it was doused by something else. Sadness? He wasn't sure. He only knew that he wanted to fix it.

Shiloh pulled in a breath. "Cash, I don't know how to tell you this. I feel like I've really jerked you around a lot, but that wasn't ever anything I meant to do. As someone told me recently, sometimes life just pulls us in whatever direction it wants, whether we give it permission to, or not."

He leaned forward and put his hands on the table, wanting to reach out and touch her, but resisting. His wolf called out for her, knowing that breathtaking dragon that was locked inside her was a part of him. "That's something I can understand."

"Good." She nodded and swiped a hand over her face, taming a strand of hair behind her ear. "I hope you really are as understanding as you mean to be. The thing is...I...oh, Cash." Shiloh put her head in her hand, resting her elbow on the table.

Now he did reach across, daring to trace the tip of her finger across her forearm. It was a small gesture, and not nearly what he wanted to do, but it sent a zing of energy up his arm just to have the barest hint of contact with her. "You can tell me, Shiloh. Think of all that we've gone through. You can tell me."

She jerked her head up and looked directly into his eyes. "I'm pregnant with your child, Cash."

The world froze. His lips parted as he saw the sincerity in her eyes, but also the fear. His breathing got faster as his wolf reached out, searching for her dragon and the other being that must also be in there. He swore he could sense the baby, and it sent his heart soaring. He pulled her hand down so he could hold it. "You are? We are?"

"Yes. I'm sorry that I didn't tell you earlier. I've known for a while. I just...I just wasn't sure what you'd think or what to do." She twined her fingers through his.

Those words sent a chill of caution up Cash's

spine. "What to do," he repeated. "I guess that's the question. What do you want to do?" At her hesitation, he decided this was his one and only chance to charge forward. "Because I can tell you exactly what I want to do. First, I want to scoop you right up off that seat and kiss you until my lips are tired. Then I want to find a gorgeous little home, something with a bit of acreage so we can get this kid a pony and give it a proper upbringing. And I want to live there with you for the rest of my life, listening to you giving me sassy retorts every time I come home late from work or turn the TV up too loud. And when we're old and gray and we have to move to a smaller place because we can't handle that house anymore, I want to turn to some young couple and tell them to go for it, because you never know what you might lose if you don't." He held his breath as he finished, both mortified and thrilled to have just said all that.

A tentative smile wriggled across her lips. "All that? Right off the cuff?"

He nodded, knowing now that everyone he'd talked to had been right. Cash had been a complete idiot for thinking otherwise. "All that, and plenty more. Shiloh, I know you have plans for your life. I know you didn't get the chance to live it the way you wanted to, and you deserve so much after taking care of your aunt and staying with her. But I do want to be with you, and I don't think that being together has to mean you can't find yourself."

She arched an eyebrow, even though there were still tears in her eyes. "So you're not upset about the baby?"

Laughter bubbled up from deep inside him, but not because any of this was funny. He was just so happy to feel that she was finally reaching out for him just as much as he was for her. Even in a restaurant in the middle of town, he knew her dragon was truly responding and feeling that link. "Upset? No. More like thrilled. Exhilarated. Stoked. I don't know. I'll have to get a thesaurus to figure it all out. But what do *you* want, Shiloh? That's what I want to know more than anything."

"I've thought about that a lot." She looked down at their linked hands, running her fingertips across his palm. "Sometimes, I felt trapped when I was living with Adelaide. I had a responsibility to her, just as she did to me. I wanted to figure out what it meant to be completely free. The thing is, I'm starting to realize that maybe being free isn't nearly as fun as I thought it would be. I like the idea of having someone to lean on, someone who will go on a wild goose chase to a mountain cabin just because he's a nice guy, someone who will go to crazy lengths that he might not be entirely comfortable with, someone who makes me realize how silly I am for ever turning him away. I want to be with you, Cash. I know now that we're supposed to be together, and it's for a good reason. I love you." Shiloh clamped her hand tightly around his.

Relief and excitement rushed through his veins. "I love you, too." A weight lifted from his shoulders as the words left his mouth. He'd tried so hard to encapsulate his feelings in other ways, but all it really required was three words. "So, what do we do now?"

"Well, I believe you did promise to kiss me until your lips got tired. We can always start with that," she replied with a sly smile.

Cash was out of his seat in a flash. He pulled her up from the table and scooped his hands underneath her, lifting her up until her lips met his. Her legs wrapped around him as he kissed her softly, his wolf and her dragon settling down with a deep sense of satisfaction at knowing they would no longer be separated. When he finally set her down again and opened his eyes, he saw Barb over by the counter. She was wiping tears from her eyes and fanning herself with a newspaper.

24

"YOU BE A GOOD GIRL, ADDY. MOMMY LOVES HER little dragon so much."

"Or wolf," Cash added. "We really won't know which she is until she's a bit older, so I hear."

"Well, whatever she is, she's just perfect." Shiloh's heart ached as the baby wrapped her fist around her mother's finger and grinned. "Oh, Addy, you're not making this any easier."

"She'll be fine," Cash assured her as he rubbed his big, rough hand across the top of Shiloh's back. "Besides, I've been looking forward to this for a long time."

"What? Fishing up in the mountain lakes?" she teased as she unsnapped the car seat from its base.

"Right. Fishing. That's exactly what I'm going to

do when I get a weekend with you all to myself." Cash kissed the back of her neck, trailing his lips up to her ear and taking a little nibble of her earlobe.

"And what if *I* want to go fishing?" she asked as she picked up Addy's car seat and looped the handle over her arm.

Cash grabbed the diaper bag from the floorboard. "You'd rather go fishing than roll around naked in bed with me all weekend? That's fine. Then we'll just go fishing naked and see where things go from there. I'm sure I can find some tackle you can use." He waggled his eyebrows suggestively.

Shiloh gave him a playful slap on the arm and laughed. "I bet you can."

Wade opened the door as they approached. The cowboy sagged his shoulders and rolled his eyes. "Here I am, getting stuck with everyone else's kids again. Lucky me." But he reached out to take the car seat from Shiloh as they walked in the door, bringing the baby up close to his face and cooing at her.

"Lucky *me* is more like it," Sierra cracked as she walked into the room. "I'll have to listen to Wade's baby talk all weekend. If you come back on Sunday evening and you see his bags packed on the front step, then you'll understand why." She tickled Addy's tiny foot and grinned.

It was clear that despite their joking, the two were thrilled to have their little goddaughter over for a weekend. Shiloh had felt strange about leaving her behind, but she knew it was exactly what they needed. Life had been hectic, and it would be good to get back up into the mountains for a while.

After their final goodbyes and several reminders as to how many bottles Addy was going through these days, the couple wound their way up into the mountains. Cash kept his hand on Shiloh's knee as she looked out the window, glad that she could finally think of this place as a getaway instead of Rapunzel's tower. She ran her hand over his arm and slipped her fingers down between his as the trees flashed by.

"Hang on," he said when he pulled up in front of the cabin. Cash jumped out of the driver's seat and came around so that he could lift Shiloh straight into his arms. She wrapped her arms around his neck as he nudged the door shut with his knee and headed for the door.

"What about our bags?" she asked with a laugh, loving the feeling of his strong arms underneath her.

It was as close to flying as she'd ever felt in her human form, as though it took him no effort at all.

Cash pressed his lips to hers at the bottom of the steps. He tipped his head and ran his tongue along her neck before devouring her mouth. His hands tightened around her, and Shiloh felt her body surging toward his. Her nipples hardened and her heart raced as he twined her fingers in the soft hairs at the back of her neck.

He pulled away, leaving her yearning for more. Cash grinned. "I think the bags can wait."

They headed into the cabin, Cash still carrying her as they crossed the threshold. "So chivalrous, Sir Cash," she teased, even though she loved it.

"I take pride in doing as my lady pleases," he replied as he kicked the door shut with his foot and headed toward the bedroom.

"Aren't you going to put me down?" Shiloh asked with a giggle.

Cash shouldered his way into the bedroom and laid her down on the bed. He moved down to her feet, removing her shoes and massaging her soles and ankles. His fingers were strong and knowledgeable.

Shiloh closed her eyes in sheer pleasure. "If

that's what we're doing for the entirety of this trip, then I'm not getting out of this bed."

"That works perfectly into my plans." Cash crawled up on the bed so that he straddled her, and he kissed her once again. She could feel his breathing quicken as he skimmed his hands under the hem of her shirt and slowly pushed the fabric out of the way until he could lift it over her head. His attentions moved down along her jawline to the tender spot just below her ear, along the side of her neck, and to her tender breasts. Cash expertly unclasped her bra and let it fall away as he kissed a line straight through the center of her cleavage. Her nipples were sore and sensitive, so he massaged her gently as he moved further down to her stomach.

A sigh escaped from Shiloh's mouth as Cash flicked his tongue against her navel while he unbuttoned her jeans and shimmied them off her hips. He knew her body like the back of his hand at this point. She was always busy with work, with Addy, and with planning out new adventures for them, but a look and a touch from Cash sent her sinking into the mattress with ease and pleasure. She gave herself over to him with abandon, feeling a pleasurable heat prickle under her skin as she melted into the bed.

Cash sent agony and anticipation soaring through her body as he pulled aside the black lace panties she'd bought especially for this trip. She realized she really wouldn't need them much, because the only thing she wanted to do was live in her own skin next to him. His hardness brushed against her leg as he dipped his tongue into her most sacred place, slowly drawing it up and then back down again as he tasted the pleasure that he was bringing about.

She clasped his shoulders as she tossed her head from side to side, feeling the tension building in her core. Her muscles tensed from her jaw all the way down to her feet, and she could tell the most essential one inside her was twisting itself into a knot capable of producing the most exquisite delight.

His hands skimmed along the insides of her thighs as he gently pushed them further apart and swirled his tongue against her. Cash knew all the right places, and he groaned as Shiloh bucked her hips against him.

That vibration was enough to push her over the edge. The climax bloomed inside her and sent spasms shooting down her legs. Shiloh bucked her hips against the deluge of rapture that'd taken over her body, her breath coming in gasps as Cash pushed her over the brink again and again. Her thighs clamped against his shoulders, and he kneaded his fingers into her flesh.

He finally pulled away, his chest heaving. Shiloh fanned herself with one hand as she smiled up at him. Any doubts she'd had about leaving for the weekend had been completely erased. Cash moved up on top of her. His arousal, already dripping with anticipation, pulsed against her sensitive folds for a moment before he slowly plunged inside.

Shiloh nearly cried out again. He'd already brought her to her peak, but having him inside her was the most ultimate satisfaction. She spread her legs wide to accommodate him as he sank his cock inside her, their skin already slick with sweat and making them stick together as their hips worked in unison. They rose and fell, their bodies both rioting inside, yet working as one. Cash's arms tensed on either side of her as he picked up his pace. Shiloh clamped herself around him, wanting to feel every moment of his pleasure. Her body remembered his attentions and easily brought her around to her climax once again just as Cash let out a howl of pleasure. She could feel her walls rippling around him, drawing out everything he had to give.

Sweaty and spent, Cash collapsed next to her on

the bed. He wrapped one arm around her and pulled her close, laying his cheek on her shoulder.

Shiloh smiled and traced her fingers on his face. “Is that all you’ve got, cowboy?”

He looked up at her with one eye. “Trust me, my beautiful dragon. I’ll never be done with you.”

THE END

If you enjoyed *Her Deputy Wolf,* you’ll love *Her Rancher Wolf!* Read on for a preview of Colton’s story.

COLTON

"You sure you're in the right place, honey?" the man on the next barstool asked.

Willa Jacobson recoiled at the man's whiskey breath. He'd obviously been there drinking for far too long, and he was leaning so close that she wanted to dive off the other side of her stool. "Excuse me?"

He grinned as his eyes swam up and down her body. "You know, pretty little thing like you, out here with all these ruffians. They're practically wolves in here."

"I'm sure." Considering that she sat in a place called the Full Moon Saloon, Willa didn't doubt it. She hadn't really cared what the place was called. She'd had a long drive up from Longmont, Colorado.

Even though she'd be getting up early the next morning for her job interview, the temptation of a nice cold beer was too good to pass up. It didn't hurt that the saloon was just down the street from her hotel, either.

"Harley!" a sharp voice snapped from the other side of the bar. The scar that ran down one side of the bartender's face, forcing his mouth into a permanent frown, made him intimidating. The effect was intensified now that he was glaring at the man who was leering at her. "What have I told you about harassing women in my bar?"

Harley sank a little on his stool. "That you won't tolerate it," he moped. "But I wasn't—"

The bartender pointed toward the door. "Out. You can come back another day when you're sober."

Though he looked like he wanted to argue, Harley slid off his stool and left.

"I'm sorry about that," the bartender said to Willa. He eyed her carefully as though he were assessing her. "Are you in town for business or vacation?"

She blinked, surprised that this man would automatically know she was from out of town. "Hopefully, business. I have a job interview tomorrow."

He gave a single, curt nod of understanding.

"You're welcome here. Just don't let trash like that bother you. If you have trouble with a single person in here, you come to me. The name's Shaw."

"Thanks. I'm Willa." She hadn't expected such strange courtesy, and even though she didn't think of herself as the type of woman who needed protection from pervs, she appreciated it. "Can I ask you something?"

Another brusque nod from Shaw.

"Is there anyone I could talk to about the cattle ranching industry around Sheridan? I've done some research online, but that's not the same as talking to someone in person."

Shaw gestured to a table off to the side, where three men sat. "They should be able to tell you anything you need to know."

"Thank you." Willa knew it was bold, but she slid off her stool and approached their table. Considering the way Shaw had treated Harley, she had a good idea that these men were safe to talk to. It didn't hurt that one of them wore the uniform of a sheriff's deputy.

Two of them looked up at her as she approached, but the deputy was lost in his own conversation. "He kept trying to tell me he wasn't there, but I'd seen it on the surveillance footage. It was impossible to deny. Oh, sorry." He said this last part as he noticed Willa standing there. "Is there something we can help you with?"

"I hope so." She ran her thumb over the condensation on her glass. "I'm looking for someone who can tell me a bit about the cattle ranching industry in this area. Shaw said you were the guys to talk to."

The man who sat alone on one side of the table nodded toward the open seat next to him, his blazing blue eyes penetrating hers right to her core. "What is it that you want to know?"

"I have a job interview tomorrow at a local ranch," Willa explained, glad that she'd found some locals to talk to. If she was going to be living there, then she would need to start getting to know people. "I'm just trying to find some information about this guy before I go and work for him. His name is Colton Ward."

A silence descended over the three men for a moment, but the man next to her was the first to nod his head. "We've heard of him, but I'm not sure what there is to know," he said as he took a long sip of his beer.

Willa lifted a shoulder. "What little I could find about him online mentioned him being a real asshole to work for. Is that true?"

"Yep," came the instant reply from the man who sat across the table. He reached out his hand. "My name is Bryce, by the way."

"Willa Jacobson."

"Cash Taylor." The deputy followed suit and then looked pointedly at Blue Eyes.

"Roger," he said as he took her hand.

Willa felt a jolt of energy sizzle across her tongue as soon as she touched him. He was handsome, that was for sure, but he definitely didn't look like a Roger. "It's nice to meet all of you."

Bryce cleared his throat. "Anyway, you said you heard this guy is an asshole. So why would you bother coming to work for him?"

That was a reasonable question. "The ranch I was working for in Longmont shut down, and I thought it was time to look for something bigger. I've heard that Colton Ward runs the best ranch in Wyoming, so I figured I'd give it a shot."

"Anything else you've heard about this rancher?" Roger asked.

"No, but I think that's what's bothering me. I could barely find anything about him online. Who in the world doesn't have a web presence these days, right?"

Roger nodded slowly, his eyebrows raised. "That's a fair point."

Cash drained the last of his beer and stood. "I've got to get home to my family. Willa, I hope you enjoy your time in Sheridan. If there's anything you need —anything at all—feel free to ask for me at the sheriff's department." He glanced at Roger before leaving.

Bryce looked uncomfortable, as though he couldn't quite decide what he should do. "I, um, I need to go talk to Shaw about some things. I'll catch you later."

"Did I scare them off?" Willa asked with a smile as she watched them go.

"Don't mind them," Roger assured her. "Cash has a baby at home, so we're lucky if we see him out anyway. As for Bryce, well, he's just Bryce. Now, tell me more about this rancher. Why did you want to find information about him online so badly?" He'd turned in his seat to face her so that one elbow rested against the back of it and the other on the table.

Those piercing eyes threw her off for a moment, but Willa recovered herself quickly. "I just thought I might be able to prepare myself for the interview if I knew him a little better."

He rubbed the back of his neck. "So if you can't find out anything about him, you just have to give him all the right answers when he interviews you."

"Like what?"

"Tell him you ran the number one cattle ranch in Colorado until your evil uncle conspired with all your ranch hands to mutiny. You had to leave the state, but you fed yourself by joining the circus as an equestrian gymnast. That'll impress anyone."

"Is that so?" Willa said with a laugh. "And here I was thinking I should just be honest and tell him about my years of experience, my love of life in the saddle, and that I'm not afraid of blood, sweat, or dirt."

Roger tipped his head to the side. "I guess that's okay, too, but I still think you should go with my idea. It'll make you far more interesting."

Her cheeks were starting to hurt from smiling so much. She'd only planned to ask for a bit of information, but the next thing she knew, they were diving into a whole conversation. Shaw brought them another round of beers as Roger told her about the best places to go in Sheridan, as well as the best places to stay away from. He approved of her hotel choice, but he told her she could've gotten a better rate if she'd spoken to someone different.

The next thing Willa knew, it was well past midnight. “Oh, no! I’ve got to get into bed. This Colton guy said I have to show up at the crack of dawn because that’s when he’s best at conducting his business.”

“You sound like you don’t approve,” Roger noted.

Willa slid her empty glass away from her and stood up. “I was actually kind of glad. To me, that’s been the only thing that seems normal about him.”

“Can I walk you back to the hotel?”

Willa smiled. She’d enjoyed spending this evening with Roger, even if she’d stayed up far too late and was going to look like a raccoon in the morning from lack of sleep. At least her appearance didn’t have anything to do with whether or not she got the job. “Sure.”

Sheridan was still in full swing, with the bars packed and groups of men and women heading down the sidewalk from one club to another. “I didn’t realize it would be like this here, with so much going on.”

Roger nodded. “There’s plenty to do here, whether you’re looking for nightlife or if you want to spend your days hiking in the Big Horns. Maybe we could do something together sometime.”

Her throat tightened, and Willa felt excitement

shooting through her body. She had planned to go to Sheridan for a job, not a man, but she couldn't say she minded. It just meant there was even more for her to look forward to while she was there. They'd already reached the parking lot of the hotel, and she hardly thought she'd be able to sleep that night. "Yeah, I'd like that."

"Good. Then I'll be in touch. I've got an early appointment in the morning, too, so I'd better get home."

Her eyes drifted up to his, and the exchange they shared with a mere glance thundered through her body like hoofbeats. The next thing she knew, Roger had pulled her into his arms for a kiss, his lips soft but determined. When she tipped her head back, he tangled his strong hands in her hair and deepened the kiss. It took her breath away, but Willa didn't want it back.

When he finally let go and held her at arm's length, those eyes just as intense out there in the dim light as they'd been in the saloon, Willa was glad she'd come to Sheridan, no matter what happened with her job interview. "I haven't been kissed like that in...well, I don't know how long."

"Glad to oblige," Roger said with a smile. "I'll see you around, Willa."

She slowly walked into the hotel and up to the hotel room, her body buzzing with excitement. It wasn't until she was tucked in bed, still far too awake to even entertain the idea of sleep, that she realized she hadn't given him her number.

ALSO BY MEG RIPLEY

ALL AVAILABLE ON AMAZON

Shifter Nation Universe

Fated Over Forty Series

Wild Frontier Shifters Series

Special Ops Shifters: L.A. Force Series

Special Ops Shifters: Dallas Force Series

Special Ops Shifters Series (original D.C. Force)

Werebears of Acadia Series

Werebears of the Everglades Series

Werebears of Glacier Bay Series

Werebears of Big Bend Series

Dragons of Charok Universe

Daddy Dragon Guardians Series

Shifters Between Worlds Series

Dragon Mates: The Complete Dragons of Charok Universe Collection (Includes Daddy Dragon Guardians and Shifters Between Worlds)

More Shifter Romance Series

Beverly Hills Dragons Series

Dragons of Sin City Series

Dragons of the Darkblood Secret Society Series

Packs of the Pacific Northwest Series

Compilations

Forever Fated Mates Collection

Shifter Daddies Collection

Early Novellas

Mated By The Dragon Boss

Claimed By The Werebears of Green Tree

Bearer of Secrets

Rogue Wolf

ABOUT THE AUTHOR

Steamy shifter romance author Meg Ripley is a Seattle native who's relocated to New England. She can often be found whipping up her next tale curled up in a local coffee house with a cappuccino and her laptop.

Download *Alpha's Midlife Baby,* the steamy prequel to Meg's Fated Over Forty series, when you sign up for the Meg Ripley Insiders newsletter!

Sign up by visiting www.authormegripley.com

Connect with Meg

amazon.com/Meg-Ripley/e/B00Z8I9AXW
tiktok.com/@authormegripley
facebook.com/authormegripley
instagram.com/megripleybooks
bookbub.com/authors/meg-ripley
goodreads.com/megripley

Printed in Great Britain
by Amazon

62237659R00150